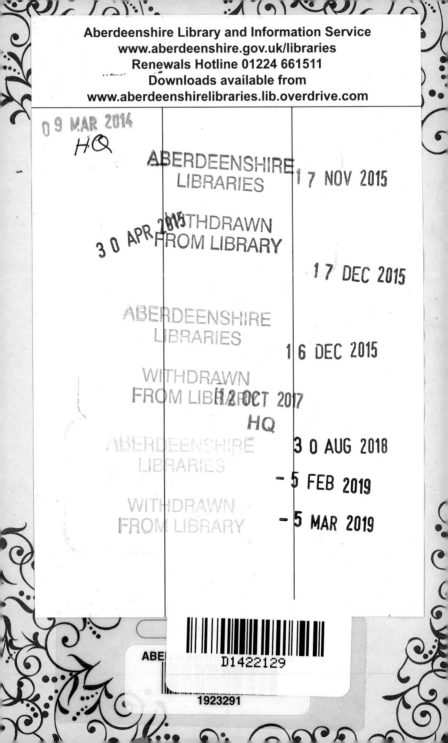

Whenever I think of 'The Incident' at Ironbridge High School — the one everyone remembers but pretends they don't — I get a horrible feeling in my stomach. Like nerves, but a lot worse. More painful. I feel ashamed of my behaviour, and yet I was also standing up for myself which can't be a completely bad thing. Right?

I just wish people would forget for real — like, have their minds magically wiped or something — rather than have to pretend it didn't happen. I think that maybe people don't want to remember it — events that can't easily be explained are best left well alone.

The Iron Witch

KAREN MAHONEY

CORGI BOOKS

THE IRON WITCH
A CORGI BOOK 978 0 552 56381 9

Published in Great Britain by Corgi Books,
an imprint of Random House Children's Boo[...]
A Random House Group Company

This edition published 2011

1 3 5 7 9 10 8 6 4 2

YA

The Random House Group Limited supports The Forest Stewardship
Council (FSC), the leading international forest certification organisation.
All our titles that are printed on Greenpeace approved FSC certified paper
carry the FSC logo. Our paper procurement policy can be found at
www.rbooks.co.uk/environment.

Mixed Sources
Product group from well-managed
forests and other controlled sources
www.fsc.org Cert no. TT-COC-2139
© 1996 Forest Stewardship Council
FSC

Corgi Books are published by Random House Children's Books,
61–63 Uxbridge Road, London W5 5SA

www.kidsatrandomhouse.co.uk
www.rbooks.co.uk

Addresses for companies within The Random House Group Limited
can be found at: www.randomhouse.co.uk/offices.htm

THE RANDOM HOUSE GROUP Limited Reg. No. 954009

A CIP catalogue record for this book is available from the British Library.

Printed and bound in Great Britain by Clays Ltd, St Ives plc.

To Mum, for always believing in me no matter what;
I love you very much.

And to Veej, for pushing me to live my dreams
(for everyone!); "thank you" doesn't even begin to cover it.

My father died saving my life when I was seven years old.

I wish I found it easier to remember him outside of my dreams—where of course he is tall and handsome, and over and over again saves me from the Wood Monster.

In my nightmares, I'm always running through twisted woodland. The trees bend close together and whisper beneath the moonlight as I stumble between them, trying desperately to keep my footing. Behind me I can hear quicksilver footsteps and a cacophony of cackling and screeching. I enter a small clearing with the yammering sound of my pursuers still ringing in my ears.

The ashen stump of a tree trunk stands in the center, a fairy-tale woodcutter's axe stuck into the top of it at an angle. I'm breathing hard, my chest burns, and the fear is like a frozen claw gripping me so tight it hurts. My child's hands reach for the scarred axe handle, even as I know I won't be able to pull it free.

I never can.

I'm surrounded by a weird choir of voices, inhumanly singing my downfall, though I can't see anything outside the clearing but trees and darkness. There are other sounds, too: strange clicks and scrapings that hurt my ears and set my teeth on edge.

And that's when my father appears, right there beside me. This part is always so clear that I can't help wondering if this is how it really happened. Dad reaches for the axe and easily yanks it out of the stump, sparing me a glance. I see the flash of familiar determination in his eyes. Maybe we will get out of here after all. Maybe it will be okay.

"Get behind me, Donna."

I do what he tells me, and as I cower behind my father's broad back I begin to pray.

But when the screeching hoard breaks into the clearing, two of them riding on the back of the Wood Monster, I stop praying and begin to scream.

One

It all started with the party.

That's what Donna Underwood would tell herself in the days that followed. If only she hadn't let Nav talk her into going with him, then maybe everything would be different. Maybe things wouldn't have gotten quite so bad.

But Donna was a total pushover when it came to her best friend, Navin Sharma. All he had to do was gaze mournfully at her with those big brown eyes and she'd gladly follow him into Hell. Or in this case, into a strange house filled with a bunch of kids who thought she was the world's biggest freak.

Which was pretty much the same thing.

It was hardly her idea of a fun way to spend Saturday night in Ironbridge, especially not when most of this crowd was still attending the high school she'd been kicked out of last year. But Navin was determined to attend the "hottest party" this side of Thanksgiving, and he had been equally determined that she should go with him. This would be more than just a regular gathering, he'd assured her gleefully; it was a major event organized by some guy who'd graduated from Ironbridge High and already dropped out of college. His parents were disgustingly loaded—and on vacation—and the party had been talked about for weeks. Apparently, *everyone* would be there.

Which was exactly what she was afraid of.

Once inside, Donna grabbed the first opportunity to make herself as inconspicuous as possible. She found a dark corner of the living room and leaned awkwardly against the wall, fiddling with her silver scarf, retying it for what felt like the hundredth time. With her embroidered blue jeans, black and silver T-shirt, and long, black velvet gloves, she looked a lot more sparkly than she felt. It didn't help that she'd already begun the day unsettled and jittery, woken by the familiar weight of cold dread. The dreams always left her that way.

Earlier that evening, she and Navin had jumped off the bus at Central Station and set off in the direction of the Grayson townhouse. As the city closed in around them, all energy and iron, Donna had felt the thrum of power beneath her feet. Her adrenaline spiked, and the accompanying rush of blood left her light-headed. Her iron-laced hands and arms throbbed in unison to the beat of the city's heart. And she knew that if she wanted to, she could shatter the bones of Navin's hand without breaking a sweat.

Donna was marked by magic. And not just any magic, but an ancient alchemical magic that had lain hidden behind legends for centuries. Yet knowing what she could do didn't make her feel special. It didn't make her feel powerful. All it did was make her feel completely and utterly alone.

But she wasn't alone tonight; she was letting Navin pull her through the streets while trying to pretend she wasn't completely terrified. Her fingers curled reflexively inside her favorite gloves as she resisted the temptation to flee.

"Stop being so cranky, Underwood. You're just nervous." Navin could barely keep the amusement out of his voice. He patted the back of her hand before releasing her.

Donna scowled. "What the hell have I got to be nervous about?"

Navin gave her his best "duh" look.

She punched him playfully on the shoulder, harder than she'd intended to. Her gloves might hide her tattoos—those strange symbols she refused to show even to Navin—but they did nothing to hide how strong she really was. Just one of the many secrets she was forced to keep. "The public story" about her arms and hands was that she'd had multiple skin grafts after being burnt in a fire. She hated the lies, but it wasn't as though she'd had much choice (that's what she tried to tell herself, anyway). And she always had to be so careful not to show her strength; she'd spent the last three years of living next door to Navin terrified that she'd do something to hurt him.

"Ow! Take it easy, Wonder Girl." Navin rubbed his biceps, then flexed it to show off his impressive lack of muscle.

"Sorry." Donna couldn't resist grinning. Navin was such an idiot sometimes, and she loved him for it. Still, despite their closeness, there was so much she hadn't told him about her family and about the Order of the Dragon. Like ... pretty much *all* of it. And not because she wasn't supposed to tell (which she wasn't), but because she wanted to protect him.

He slung an easy arm around her shoulders as they crossed the street, making it just before the *Don't Walk* sign flashed back up. "Come on, Don. Something's up, I know you too well."

She shrugged, unable to meet his eyes.

"Don't panic—I'm not going to interrogate you right now. You can tell me all about it at the party."

Donna grimaced. "I can't wait."

Navin fixed her with a mock glare. "You just don't want to go."

She pulled a face. "No, *really*? Partying with the 'elite' isn't exactly my idea of a good time, and they're not going to be happy when I walk through the door. You're taking your reputation in your hands being seen at a party with me."

"So young, and yet so cynical."

"It's true and you know it."

Navin laughed. "What 'reputation' have I got to worry about? I slip under a lot of people's cool-dar, that's all. I'm different, but not different enough for them to bother with tormenting me."

"Like they do with me, you mean." Donna pouted.

He steered her past a homeless guy, wearing an AC/DC T-shirt and a ratty, floor-length coat, standing in the middle of the sidewalk. Other pedestrians flowed by him like water around a stone. "Come on, stop feeling sorry for yourself."

"Can we leave when I'm not having fun anymore?" Donna hoped she didn't sound as needy and vulnerable as she felt.

"Sure, we can leave. Of course, that means you actually have to *have* some fun before we can even consider going home…" Navin ruffled her hair and grinned, ducking so she couldn't hit him again.

That same grin now beamed across the dimly lit room at her, a room crowded with teenagers having that elusive "fun." Donna pulled back her shoulders and lifted her chin, scanning the clusters of kids she vaguely knew but wished she didn't. She'd spent most of her life trying to fit in, but it was so much harder ever since "the Incident." In the wake of that event, she'd left Ironbridge High to be home-schooled by the Order ... everyone considered it best that she only appear for exams, and special arrangements had been made. And so here she was now, surrounded by a bunch of kids she once knew, kids who thought she was the worst kind of loser. A loser with a capital *L*. A freak.

Although it was a totally hopeless task, Donna had promised Nav she would at least *try* to blend into this scene. And it wasn't like she had anything else to do. She'd rather be home right now with Aunt Paige, but her aunt was on a business trip to Boston and wouldn't be back until late.

Navin caught her eye from across the room again and smiled, white teeth flashing against his burnt cinnamon skin. His black hair was neat today, smoothed straight back and falling to the collar of his ever-present, black and red, fake leather biker's jacket (apparently a mandatory accessory for riding his beaten-up old bicycle through the busy Ironbridge streets like he was on a Motocross track).

Nodding and trying to return his smile, Donna hoped Navin hadn't noticed how miserable she was. She didn't want to spoil this for him. But honestly, why did he bother? Her ex–school friends would never accept her. In fact, she'd been offered proof of this the minute they'd walked through the front door of the party. The first thing Melanie Swan had said to her—*about* her, more accurately—was directed to Navin. "What did you have to bring the *freak* for?"

It was only Navin's restraining hand on her arm that had stopped Donna from shoving the bottle of whatever Melanie was drinking straight down the girl's throat. Or perhaps somewhere even more painful, she reflected grimly. Navin had glanced a warning at her, then taken the inexplicably popular class president to task for being nasty to a good friend of his. "I would've expected more from you, Mel," he'd said, his voice unusually sharp. "You're supposed to be setting an example. And I mean, a good one."

Unbelievably, Melanie had eaten it up and apologized. To Navin, of course, not to Donna herself. She'd twiddled her bright blonde hair and started acting almost girly around him.

Donna had felt a stab of irritation. Was she flirting with him? Gross.

Shaking her head to clear it of that unpleasant image, Donna reached for the nearest drink, then realized it had alcohol in it and put it back down again. She didn't want to go against Aunt Paige's rules tonight, especially when it was so important to keep a clear head. She couldn't afford to lose her temper again and give these people more reason to hate her. Not because she cared what they thought; if she never saw any of them ever again, it would be too soon. But she cared for Navin's sake.

People like Melanie Swan made it so hard, though.

The crush of bodies and voices was overwhelming. The music beat a steady rhythm in Donna's temples and through the soles of her feet. Excited students greeted each other with high-pitched shrieks or back-slapping, accompanied by whoops and hollers. Jettisoning any idea she might have had of "fitting in," Donna worked her way over to Navin. She hung around the edges of his conversations for a while ... for as long as she could bear to feel like a burden.

It was time to make her escape. Thinking that maybe it would be quieter on the top floor, Donna yelled in Navin's ear that she was going to find a bathroom. When he'd understood and nodded, she left him to his shouted conversation with a couple of wannabe bikers. Head ringing, she moved away from the boom of the speakers, squeezed past a couple making out on the main stairway, and worked her way up to the top floor.

Things were just as crowded here as they had been downstairs. Bedroom doors were closed, and she could hear sounds behind them that made her blush and step quickly away. There was a line for the bathroom, headed by some shrill girls she used to know. Ducking into the only open doorway in an effort to avoid her ex-classmates, Donna hoped she wasn't walking in on anything she'd rather not witness.

Thankfully, the bedroom was empty. A feeling of peace descended on her, and she wondered how this haven of quiet had escaped the hordes of partiers.

Then Donna's fingers tingled, and for a moment she thought she could sense magic.

She froze, just inside the doorway, and tried to quiet her mind while allowing her senses to reach out further than might be considered...normal. When you'd grown up surrounded by magic, it was hard *not* to develop a sensitivity to it. It was no wonder that the members of the Order were so keen to train her in their ancient alchemical arts.

After a moment, Donna closed the door behind her and looked around for signs of anything *other*. Things felt pretty ordinary now, and she wondered if she'd imagined that whisper of magic.

The bedroom was quite masculine, done out in cappuccino and chocolate tones, with earthy rusts thrown in for contrast in the curtains and lamps. The lights were on, but dimmed to a warm glow. There was a black guitar gathering dust in one corner, like some relic of an emo adolescence, and a desk in the other corner, on which sat what looked like a very expensive computer. The walk-in closet hidden behind dark double doors was probably huge, and there was even an en-suite bathroom.

Donna felt a cool breeze caress the back of her neck and shivered, wishing she still had her coat on. Peeking behind one of the heavy curtains, she saw a set of ornate French doors. One of the doors stood slightly ajar. Further investigation revealed a small balcony and an iron stepladder that lead toward the roof.

Why not?

She could use some air, even if it was chilled, near-winter air. Tugging her gloves up as far as they'd go—almost covering her elbows—Donna slipped out onto the tiny balcony and gripped the metal railings.

She pulled herself up onto the first step, feeling unsteady on what was little more than a fire escape. Her sequinned sneakers squeaked on the rungs and she could hear distant traffic passing beneath her feet. As she approached the top and realized just how high up she really was, she had a dizzying moment of vertigo. Her gloves slipped on the metal rungs and she held on tight, for once grateful for the magically enhanced strength in her hands.

And then a head poked over the edge of the roof. Donna found herself inches away from the striking face of a young guy who'd obviously found the same escape route she had. His dark blond hair seemed bright under the clear night sky.

"I wondered how long it would take for someone to come and ruin the peace and quiet up here," he drawled, in a flat, bored sort of voice.

Donna saw the hand-rolled cigarette in his fingers, at the same time catching a whiff of something sweet and sickly. It reminded her of when her aunt burnt sage to cleanse the house.

"Well, come on then, if you're going to," he added. He placed the cigarette in the corner of his mouth and extended both hands.

Donna had a moment of doubt, suddenly wishing she were back downstairs with Navin. But she shook it off. Surely sitting with this guy couldn't be any worse than hanging out with Melanie and her clones.

She allowed herself to be pulled the rest of the way up onto the roof.

Two

Donna sat on a narrow bench bolted to the roughly hewn roof-deck. Her new companion sat at her feet, directly on the platform built onto the roof, leaning against what looked like a protective railing. She shifted uncomfortably in the silence and watched him as he flicked away the butt of whatever he'd been smoking.

He tilted his head until they were looking into one another's eyes.

Donna's chest felt tight, and a strange, watery feeling sloshed around in her stomach. His eyes were the greenest she had ever seen. Viridian-bright, but with textures swirling within that looked like fresh moss on the bark of a tree. She wondered if he was cold in his thin lilac shirt (and how many guys could get away with *that* color?), then saw a black sweater discarded at his side. His toffee-colored hair was a shade or two lighter than hers, short at the back and longer on top so that it fell choppily into those otherworldly eyes. His skin was smooth and golden, as if he'd just returned from vacation.

"Aren't you scared of falling?" Donna almost jumped at the sound of her own voice.

Just for a second, the guy looked as though he might smile. Instead, he leaned his head back, resting it against the peeling, black-painted iron railing. He stared straight up into the star-filled sky.

"Well?" Donna prodded. "Aren't you?"

"No."

"Oh."

She continued to watch him. Why had she even come up here? This whole evening had been a huge mistake.

But she couldn't help gazing at his wide mouth, with its full bottom lip, and letting her imagination go crazy. She had a sudden picture in her head of kissing this unknown boy. Well, not exactly a *boy*... he looked older than her by at least a couple of years. She knew that his lips would be soft but insistent, that lazy half-smile suddenly transformed into something more intense.

She shook her head, squeezing her eyes tightly shut, then looked back at him. His eyebrows were raised in what could have been either curiosity or amusement—Donna couldn't tell which. She blushed, and instantly hated herself for having such a childish reaction.

"What were you thinking about just then?"

Donna pulled her knees up against her chest and wrapped her arms around them. "Nothing."

"Nothing. Right." He made that last word stretch out for a lot longer than was polite.

Donna tossed her hair and looked away, clenching her black-gloved hands into fists against her jeans.

His burst of laughter took her by surprise. What surprised her even more was that the next moment they were laughing together. She wondered how she knew that he was someone who laughed as rarely as she did. It felt like he knew this too, and that they were sharing a secret moment of humor they could hide from other people, keep just between the two of them—strangers united in an unspoken contract of...*something*. It was exhilarating and scary.

Getting her breathing back under control, Donna looked over at her companion once more. "So, what's your name?"

"Xan. Yours?"

"I'm Donna. Underwood." She cringed inwardly at the sound of her voice. Why did she always have to sound so *young*? "Is your name short for Alexander?"

"Ah. Beautiful *and* wise, this Donna Underwood."

She could have felt offended at his tone, but she noticed the glint in his eyes and decided it was nice to be teased by someone other than Navin.

"You're not enjoying the party, then?" she asked.

"I should hope not."

"What's that supposed to mean?"

He shifted his position slightly, making it easier for him to look up at her. "Well, it wouldn't do to enjoy one's own party, would it?"

Donna found herself blushing again. "Oh, you're Alexander Grayson."

"Pleased to meet you," he replied, smiling that strange half-smile again. "I'd be even more pleased if you'd come down here with me. I'm getting an appalling crick in my neck."

She wanted to say something cool and sophisticated, maybe even ask him why he wanted to sit on the edge of the roof, why he couldn't come join her on the bench instead, but there was something in his voice that made her hesitate ... a vulnerability hovering just beneath the surface that made her wonder about him. She slid down onto the platform and tried to figure out where he was from. He had a vaguely British accent, it seemed, with a touch of Bostonian around the vowels and maybe something else, too. Something a little more exotic.

She tucked her legs beneath her and settled down a short distance from Xan.

"That's better," he said. "It's not as cold once you get down here."

Donna did feel cold. She was acutely aware of her short sleeves, with only the velvet of her gloves offering the illusion of warmth. She shivered and wrapped her arms around herself tightly, feeling unbearably shy as this stranger watched.

Xan held out the sweater she'd noticed earlier. "Here, put this on."

She hesitated, but only for a moment. "Thanks." Quickly pulling the still-warm material over her head, she tried not to be too obvious as she took in the scent of the sweater's owner. Deodorant or aftershave, perhaps; cigarette smoke; and something else, something that spoke of moss and trees and wide open fields of swaying grass. Frowning, she met his curious gaze and tried to tidy her dishevelled hair.

"So," he said. "What high school do you go to?"

Hating that he'd immediately guessed her age, Donna tried to keep the frown off her face. "I don't."

He raised golden-brown eyebrows. "You're in college?"

"No, I'm home-schooled. I'm a senior. I still have to go to Ironbridge High for exams and stuff, but other than that I'm out of the rabble."

His lips quirked. "Can't blame you for that. Why home-schooled?"

"Let's just say I had a disagreement with a significant portion of the student body."

"Ah." Xan shifted so that his body turned toward her, then stretched long arms above his head and yawned loudly. Donna wasn't fooled by his lazy movements and sleepy eyes—this guy was sharp, underneath the laid-back exterior.

"What about you?" she asked.

"What *about* me?"

"You know, schools, colleges…" She let the question drift off. Maybe it would be rude to let on that she knew he'd dropped out of college.

"I went away to college last year. Things didn't work out." He fixed her with his emerald gaze. "But you probably knew that already."

She ignored the sudden blush warming her cheeks. "I'd heard something, but I don't make a habit of listening to gossip—especially because I'm usually the subject of it."

He gazed at her for a long moment. "I'd love to hear what people say about you, Donna Underwood."

She bit her lip and changed the subject. "So, what are you doing up here when the party's down there? Shouldn't you be playing host or something?"

His laugh echoed with bitterness. "Yeah, like I'm the perfect host."

"What does *that* mean?"

"Nothing. I just agree to stupid things when I'm bored."

There was silence. Donna fiddled with the sleeve of Xan's sweater. She didn't know what to say anymore, and was again regretting coming up here. She thought of Navin, downstairs with the crowd, and wished they could just go home. If she hadn't left her cell phone in her coat pocket, she'd be able to check the time. Her stomach clenched as she pictured her aunt's return home and remembered her standard weekend curfew.

"What time is it?"

Xan pulled out his cell. "Not long 'til midnight, Cinderella."

She smiled at that. "I actually do have to go soon. I only have an hour before I'm supposed to be home. And my friend is probably looking for me."

He nodded. "I hope I didn't scare you off. I can be a little—" He hesitated. "A little bit eccentric, I guess."

"Do you work at that, then?" Donna teased.

"Only when I want to impress pretty girls."

Pretty? Was this ridiculously hot guy calling *her* pretty? Donna started to get up, but his hand on her arm stopped her.

"Why do you wear the gloves?" he asked. "It's not just fashion, is it?"

Donna attempted a light tone. "You think I'd wear these for *fashion*?"

He conceded her point with a slight smile. "Seriously, though. Why?"

Her heart contracted and she found it difficult to breathe. Why did she feel so compelled to tell this guy the truth? She looked down at her covered hands. "Because I'm different," she said finally, her voice barely audible.

"Me too," he replied, almost as softly.

They looked at one another again, Donna's somber gray eyes gazing into his green. Stone and forest. Iron and leaf.

"I knew that…" she began slowly. "I know things about people, sometimes." Her intuition had always been good.

The corner of Xan's mouth quirked upwards. "What do you know about me?"

Donna closed her eyes for a moment.

Unbidden memories flooded her, pushing into her mind with a cold weight that took her breath away. Memories of a dark and whispering wood, a clearing, and the sound of death following at her heels. *Her* memories, not his. At least, she thought they were her memories.

She pushed the images away and opened her eyes to find Xan watching her with curiosity.

It had been a long time since she'd allowed herself to think about what had happened to her in the Ironwood. She dreamt of it most nights, but to see it so clearly just now, when she was awake…Donna trembled, hoping Xan didn't notice, and tried to smile.

"Well, you're tough to read," she managed to reply. Why were memories of Ironwood Forest coming to her so easily right now, when she was trying to focus on Xan? The mood had changed, and she felt as though she was on the edge of something important and scary.

"You are too, Miss Donna Underwood." He dug into a pocket and pulled out a small tin of tobacco. "Hey, do you smoke?"

"*Ew*, no way." The words were out before she could stop them.

Xan didn't seem offended. A smile tugged at the corner of his mouth as he began to open the tin. His fingers were long and tanned, and there was a fluid grace to his movements … an intense energy that made Donna feel breathless as she watched him. He wasn't like anyone she'd ever met before.

"You really are different, aren't you?" She cringed inwardly after she spoke, wondering what had possessed her to say that. Maybe it was the vulnerable look on his face. Or the way he tried to hide things, yet seemed to want to invite her into his world.

He nodded, very slowly. "I guess we all have secrets. Like you're hiding something with those gloves."

Her eyes slid away first. She couldn't do it—she just couldn't quite bring herself to reach out to this person. She'd only just met him; *what is wrong with me?* she thought. Here she was, tempted to spill the secret of how her hands had been magically remade, spill it just as easily as the kids downstairs spilled beer on the carpet. She bit her lip and kept her mouth shut.

Xan shifted to a cross-legged position and began filling a cigarette paper with tobacco. "It seems the sharing has ended." His voice had gone flat again; the drawling tone had returned.

Donna stood up too quickly and the rush of dizziness almost overwhelmed her. "I really should go. I have to get a cab."

"Of course," Xan replied, tucking the newly made cigarette behind one ear. "I'll help you climb down."

She backed away before his hovering hand could touch her. "No thanks, I can do it myself."

But he followed her anyway.

When they were back in the bedroom below, Donna didn't know what to say. Something about Xan made her feel connected, even though she knew almost nothing about him. She was often comforted by the sense of connection she felt with Navin; Navin made her feel like she actually had some semblance of a normal life (whatever that was). But this was different.

Xan was different.

Donna wriggled out of the black sweater, feeling suddenly overheated and awkward as she handed it back to Xan. Her eyes wandered to the digital clock by the side of the unmade bed. *His* bed. "Crap. I really have to go. Navin will be looking for me."

"Navin?" His eyebrows shot up. "Ah, the boyfriend." He made it a statement.

"No, just a friend." She shrugged. "My best friend, actually."

"Oh." Xan rubbed a hand across his face. "Can I call you? I think we have a lot more to talk about…" Just for a moment, he sounded uncertain of himself. It gave Donna the courage to take a chance.

"Sure." She reeled off her number and he punched buttons on his cell phone.

When Xan stepped toward her, though, she found herself wanting to run. Just who the hell *was* Alexander Grayson? But she forced herself to stand her ground. Xan reached out a hand, and she held her breath as he gently moved back a strand of hair that had fallen into her eyes, tucking it behind her ear.

Warmth spread through her body as she attempted a smile. Donna realized, for the first time, that she had to look up to meet his eyes. He was tall. Taller than Nav, she thought, and immediately felt disloyal.

Xan's hand dropped to her shoulder as they watched each other. And then his retreating fingers brushed her arm, right where the edge of her black glove met the white skin of her elbow.

There was a sudden *spark*, like static electricity—only a lot stronger.

Donna jerked away from Xan's touch as an aching filled her hands and arms. It was like a cramp, but an impossible sensation that attacked bone rather than muscle. She remembered the pain of her childhood—multiple "operations" on her disfigured arms as Maker worked on her with metal and magic, and the expression on Aunt Paige's face when she visited after each procedure.

"What the hell was that?" Xan was looking at her as if she was something both precious and dangerous. His voice was pitched low, and his eyes flashed in the dimly lit room. He rubbed his hands together as though they were cold and glanced at the half-open door.

Donna swallowed. "What was *what*?" The ache in her bones was now more like a tingling sensation that spread throughout her arms. She needed to get out of here. Whatever had just happened between them, she would think about it later, when she didn't have to breathe under the intensity of Xan's gaze.

He scowled. "You felt it too. Don't tell me you didn't feel it."

Donna took a step toward the door. "It was just an electric shock. No big deal."

For a moment, she wondered if he was actually going to try to stop her from leaving. Her heart pounded and she resisted the temptation to rub her arm.

But Alexander Grayson just stood and watched her, almost as though he might be able to look *into* her if he tried hard enough.

Donna walked quickly toward the door, glancing back only once as she let herself out. She headed downstairs in search of Navin.

Navin, predictably, was furious with her. "Where have you been? I've been searching everywhere for you. I called your phone, like, a hundred times."

Donna couldn't help thinking he sounded like a parent who'd lost his child at the shopping mall, but she managed to keep her smile under wraps. "Don't exaggerate," she replied, checking the missed calls on her cell as she tucked herself into her coat. Her eyebrows lifted when she saw just how many phone calls she'd missed. "Oh. You did call a few times, didn't you?"

"Of course I did!" Navin practically exploded. "I didn't know what to think. I started to wonder if Melanie and her minions had gotten hold of you."

His concern was touching but Donna felt strangely distant from him, as though everything was happening through a filter, like a blind had been drawn down over her emotions so she didn't have to feel things so sharply.

"I'm sorry, Nav," she said, "but what did you think Melanie would do to me? Looks like you have her eating out of the palm of your hand, anyway." There was also the fact that Melanie Swan hadn't messed with her directly since the infamous Incident. Donna tried to think of something else, yet the memory kept pushing its way up into her mind like a stubborn weed.

"Shut up, Underwood. Don't try distracting me; you're in big trouble." Navin pointed to the dial on his watch. "*Shit*. And there's going to be even bigger trouble for you if we don't get home in the next half hour."

Donna frowned. "It's not like Aunt Paige is going to boil me alive…"

"I wouldn't be too sure. Last time you came home late with me, she threatened to hex me."

"She was kidding!" Okay, so her aunt liked to cultivate a quirky alternative/New Age type of persona for those outside the Order, but sometimes Nav took it a bit too seriously. He was half-convinced that Paige was a modern witch—which wasn't a million miles from the truth. Sort of.

"Look, I *said* I was sorry for worrying you." Donna tried to steer the conversation away from her aunt.

Navin put a casual arm around her shoulders and gave her a squeeze; she knew all was forgiven. "What were you doing, anyway?"

"I was getting some air, up on the roof."

"On the *roof*?"

She smiled. "Where better?"

He shook his head, smiling faintly. "You're weird, you know that?"

Donna looked at him innocently as they headed toward the front door. "I thought that was why you hung out with me."

"Yeah, that's exactly why." Navin rolled his eyes. "Come on, I called a cab already."

She laughed and opened the front door, but hesitated when footsteps hurried down the long hallway behind them.

"Donna, hold up a sec!"

Turning around slowly, Donna saw Xan holding out her silver scarf. Her hand went to her throat; she'd been missing it for a while. Had it fallen off when they were on the roof?

Xan pushed too-long bangs out of his eyes. "You dropped this."

Navin looked between the two of them, an expression on his face that Donna had never seen before. She felt her cheeks warm and hated that she suddenly felt *guilty*. It wasn't like she'd done anything wrong.

She snatched her scarf from Xan with a mumbled acknowledgement, hoping nobody noticed how her hands were trembling. That bone-deep, weary ache had returned, making her wish she could just wrap her arms around her body and wait for the pain to pass. The sensation—like her bones were grinding together—brought sudden tears to her eyes. Blinking them away and trying to look like nothing was wrong, Donna wound the scarf around her neck with stiff fingers.

Xan smiled. "That looks good with your coat."

"Um ... thanks." She shuffled her feet and decided she would have to introduce the guys. She touched Navin's hand. "Nav, this is Xan—Alexander Grayson," she began. "We met upstairs. Xan, this is my friend Navin Sharma."

They sized each other up, the way that guys seem to do so well. Then Navin reached out his hand. "Pleased to meet you." His voice sounded anything but. What on earth's gotten into him, Donna wondered, although she was grateful to see him at least making an effort.

Xan shook Nav's hand. "Likewise. I hope you had a good time?"

"Yeah, it was cool. Thanks."

The beat from the music pumping out of the living room vibrated through the soles of Donna's sneakers. Nobody said anything as Xan switched his attention back to her. He was watching her with that strange, curious expression, as if she were a new species he'd just discovered. She wanted to tell him it was rude to stare, but there was no way she'd do that in front of Nav.

There was a crash from the main room and Xan cringed. "Bastards! Now what have they broken?"

Navin's gaze slid over to Donna and their eyes met. His eyebrows were raised, and she almost giggled. *Saved by some clumsy kids*, she thought.

"Sorry," Xan said. He ran a hand through his hair again. "I'd better see what those morons are up to."

Donna nodded. "Okay, thanks again."

Xan walked back in the direction of the ominous clattering sounds. "I'll call you," he threw over his shoulder.

Donna wanted to disappear into the alcohol pooled on the carpet. What did he have to say that for? Men were such idiots.

She glanced at Navin and was relieved to see that he didn't seem to have a reaction. Maybe he hadn't heard. Yeah, she could hope...

They let themselves out of the house. Donna toed an empty bottle out of the way and glanced across the street. She eyed the darkness; did something move? Then a skinny shadow ducked behind a wall and she almost gasped. Her mouth was suddenly dry and she stopped walking.

"What's up?" Navin had his hand on the heavy iron gate at the end of the front walk, ready to step out onto the sidewalk.

"Wait." Donna grabbed his arm; she squeezed too tightly, and winced.

Navin frowned and made a big show of rubbing his arm. He studied her face for a moment. "Donna, what is it?"

She scanned the street, swallowing past the lump in her throat. Her heart was pounding. *There! There it was again.* A small silhouette moved with uncanny grace, sliding between shadows as it climbed over the wall into the next yard.

"Did you see that? Something just went over that wall, I *saw* it." She was whispering and she knew she must sound crazy, but she couldn't help it. Whatever she'd just seen slipping through the shadows was a lot more sinister than a super-big cat.

"There's nothing there, Donna." Navin fixed her with a strange look. "Are you sure you haven't been drinking?"

"Shut up, you know I haven't."

"Actually, I have no way of knowing that, considering how you decided to spend most of the evening wandering around on the roof." He raised an eyebrow, something Donna had always wished she could do. The single-eyebrow raise was, sadly, not something she had ever been able to master. Not even with Nav's expert tutoring.

"Oh, just forget it." Donna let out the breath she hadn't realized she'd been holding. "Maybe I really *am* going nuts."

"Going nuts? I'm sorry to inform you that it's far too late for that, Underwood."

Donna resisted the temptation to demonstrate just how strong she really was. But she couldn't hold back a sigh of relief when their cab pulled up. At least Navin was teasing her again—the tension that had formed between them when Xan was around seemed to have lifted. She looked over her shoulder as she climbed into the back seat, knowing she wouldn't feel happy until they'd gotten out of there.

She was almost certain that something had been watching them from across the street. The crawling sensation in her stomach stayed with her all the way home.

Whenever I think of "the Incident" at Ironbridge High School—the one everyone remembers but pretends they don't—I get a horrible feeling in my stomach. Like nerves, but a lot worse. More painful. I feel ashamed of my behavior, and yet I was also standing up for myself, which can't be a completely bad thing. Right?

I just wish people would forget for real—like, have their minds magically wiped or something— rather than have to pretend it didn't happen. Events that can't be explained rationally are best left alone. But kids like Melanie Swan don't easily forget being made to look stupid in front of their friends.

All I wanted—all I'd ever wanted—was to get through my days at school quietly. It was bad enough being different because of wearing the gloves the whole time; just standing out that way makes you feel uncomfortable. Some students thought I was trying to make a "fashion statement" and made snide remarks about it when they thought I couldn't hear. Melanie, though, didn't care whether I could hear or not. Sometimes she would just ask me to my face, "What's up with your hands, Underwood? Trying to stop biting your nails?" Or, "How do you manage to hold a pen with those things on?" And I would blush and hate myself for it, turning away and hiding behind Navin. I tried to ignore her—managed it pretty well for almost two years.

But once people figured out the gloves weren't just for show—that I was given special permission to wear them because of something that had happened to me—Melanie's curiosity got the better of her. To be fair to her, she wasn't the only one, but there's always a ringleader with these things. I was excused from some sports activities and she hated that (she was probably born with pom-poms attached to her hands). She just couldn't stand it that I was treated differently.

Anyway, Navin wasn't at school that day for whatever reason, and I was rummaging in my locker trying to find a textbook I was sure I'd shoved in there the day before. Melanie came up behind me and pushed me so that I stumbled, banging my head on the locker.

So, I was trying to pull myself back out of my locker when I felt two pairs of hands grabbing me on either side, holding me in position so I couldn't get out and stand up straight. And then someone else grabbed my right hand and started pulling off my glove.

I still remember the rush of adrenaline that filled me. It was like a heat wave that started in my pounding heart, spread throughout my body, and made my head buzz with caged energy. I wanted their hands off me. I didn't want anyone to see my hands and arms.

I heard Melanie's voice—"Look, there's something here!" And that was it. I just lost it. I wrenched my right hand free, for a moment not even caring if the glove came off, and gripped the edges of the locker with both hands. I pushed, using all the strength in my arms and hands— pushed myself upright with such force that I threw off whoever had been holding me.

And then I stood facing Melanie Swan, and a pretty big group of friends and curious bystanders. Someone said, "Look at her locker," in an awed voice, and I swung around to look along with everyone else.

The door was open, but where I'd gripped the sides of it, you could see clear handprints indented into the metal. It was like paper that had been crumpled up without a second thought, the steel edges collapsing in on themselves.

"What kind of a freak are you, Underwood?" Melanie asked, staring at me. Her perfect blue eyes were filled with disdain and—I was pleased to note—fear. "I always knew there was something weird about you."

"Leave me alone," was all I could think to say. My hands were shaking pretty badly, but I man-

aged to close the door of my half-crushed locker, knowing there wasn't a chance in hell it would shut properly and not even caring. I just wanted an excuse to turn away from the expressions on all of those faces. The door hung at a slight angle, looking drunken and forlorn in the row of upright lockers.

But Melanie still hadn't got enough of me. I glanced around desperately, hoping for a miracle in the form of a passing teacher, but it didn't seem I was in luck that day.

She put one pale, perfectly manicured hand in the center of my chest and pushed me against the locker door. Her fingernails matched my crimson gloves. "Stay out of my way, freak."

I don't know if it was her calling me "freak" again, or if it was the slow and exaggerated way she pushed me. I don't know if I was still buzzing with adrenaline. Whatever it was, something inside of me snapped.

I stepped as close to her as I could get without treading on her delicate toes. "You've got it the wrong way around. You stay the hell out of my way."

I turned to the locker, drew back my fist, and punched it as hard as I could.

With an ear-splitting shriek of metal, the whole door collapsed inwards, wrecking the locker *beyond any hope of repair. There was a collective gasp from the small audience and I was gratified to see Melanie back up a few steps, eyes wide and staring.*

I took a few paces toward her. "That's what you'll get if you bother me again." I turned on my heel and walked away on shaking legs, not caring that people parted before me like the Red Sea. Not caring that they were shocked and afraid.

At that moment, all I gave a damn about was that I had won.

Three

Donna slouched deeper into her seat and stared out of the greasy window, barely noticing the scenery that the bus grumbled past. She didn't want to see Maker today, but her experience with Xan last night had worried her enough that she wanted to get her hands and arms checked out.

It never hurt to be careful, although it *had* hurt to get up so early on a Sunday morning.

Feeling a bit like Cinderella, she had made it home at two minutes past one last night, sneaking into the house with as much stealth as she could manage, being so tired. Aunt Paige was, thankfully, already asleep; Donna was relieved she hadn't waited up.

And then, this morning, there was no sign of her aunt apart from a note saying she had a last-minute breakfast meeting (she apologized for working on a Sunday) and that she'd be back to spend time together in the afternoon. At least it meant Donna didn't need to explain where she was going.

Late-autumn sun glanced off the bus windows, making patterns in the smeared glass. Donna idly traced the shapes with her stiff fingers—clad in purple velvet gloves today—as she watched the wide main streets of Ironbridge bump past. Tucked into a riverside nook, Ironbridge always seemed like a miniature version of Boston to Donna. It was quite charming for a small-sized city.

She closed her eyes against another sudden pain. Resting her gloved hands carefully in her lap, she waited for the spasm to pass. Maybe seeing Maker today wasn't such a bad idea. Although stiffness in her hands wasn't unusual, especially once the weather turned cold, this sharp ache was new. It made her feel old and tired, like maybe she had arthritis way too young. If Maker knew what was happening to her—what was causing these strange sensations—he might be able to fix it. That's what he did, after all: fixed things.

Donna tried to forget the cold ache in her bones and focus, instead, on the streets sweeping past. Ironbridge was like a story to her, a fairy tale filled with tricks and trials and monsters in the shadows waiting to take away everything you cared about. Since she was as good as orphaned, Donna felt like that most clichéd of fairy-tale heroines—except that her mother was still alive, living a half-life at the Institute.

At the ripe old age of seventeen, Donna had decided that "happily ever after" didn't exist for freaks like her.

The bus finally shuddered to a stop outside an industrial park. Tall, corrugated steel fencing wrapped around the property like silver packaging. Donna jumped to her feet and clattered down the narrow aisle. "Wait, I'm getting off here!" The doors had already closed, but hissed and sighed as they reluctantly re-opened for her.

"Thanks," she called back, stepping onto the dusty concrete sidewalk.

As the bus pulled away, she had a clear view across the road. It was empty, apart from an elderly woman pushing a rusty-looking shopping cart, but Donna had the strange, creeping feeling that just moments before she was being watched. Again.

Frowning, she tried to shake off the crazy new levels of paranoia that seemed to be haunting her. Just because she'd been brought up in the bosom of a secret society of centuries-old magic didn't mean that she had to let herself become as obsessed as Quentin and Simon and all the others.

Buttoning her black corduroy jacket against the chill in the air, Donna walked along the scarred and graffiti-clad fencing. Cars intermittently rushed past, even this early on a Sunday, since the industrial park was along a popular shortcut to the center of town.

She reached the rarely used side-entrance and pushed the rusty gate open as far as it would go before the heavy padlock and chain pulled taut. There was just enough room to squeeze through, if she crouched down and breathed in.

The morning sun bounced off the high, barred windows of the familiar stone warehouse. Other buildings were spread out around the lot, though some were now deserted thanks to the recession. This particular warehouse had been Maker's workshop for as long as she could remember, hidden amid the hustle and bustle of local businesses and manufacturers. Donna knew that, were it not for the injury to her hands, she would never have had a reason to come out here, never been privy to as many secrets of the Order as she was. Maker could be serious and focused at times, but he was also talkative when he worked on her. She probably knew a lot more about the alchemists than Aunt Paige would approve of.

Donna knocked on the heavy iron door and waited for a moment. There was often no reply. The old man was usually buried in some experiment or other, working weekends when everything else was quiet out here. She banged on the door once more, her hand aching, and was just about to try opening it when something brushed her shoulder.

She screamed and spun around—

"Navin!"

Navin dropped his bike with a crash of metal and stumbled backward over it. His face mirrored the shock on her own as they stared at each other.

The moment seemed to stretch on for too long. Donna's mind raced. Where had Navin come from? Had he followed her?

"What are you *doing* here?" she managed to choke out.

Navin ignored her, picking up his bike and making a big show of checking it for damage.

Donna knew him too well. "Quit stalling and start talking, Sharma. Did you *follow* me? Please don't tell me you've turned stalker, because that would not be cool."

He glared at her, his brown eyes filled with a conflicting mixture of guilt and anger. "Can you blame me? You keep so many secrets, Donna. And then when you acted all freaked out last night—"

"Oh my God, you *did* follow me!"

"Shut up, it's not like you can blame me." His shoulders were tense inside the ever-present biker jacket. "You met that guy at the party and weren't even going to tell me. What's *that* all about?"

Donna opened her mouth to reply, but immediately shut it. This wasn't going to get them anywhere. And what was she supposed to say? She settled for shoving him— harder than she knew she should, but it made her feel better.

He almost toppled over his bike again. "Dammit, woman, stop trying to beat me. I'll sue you for domestic violence."

They scowled at each other, and then Navin's mouth twitched and Donna could feel her own cold lips spread into a reluctant grin.

"*Domestic violence?* You're deluded, Sharma."

"And again, you have too many secrets, Underwood. What are you, a teenage spy?"

She almost laughed. "No, definitely not that."

Navin wheeled his bike to the side of the warehouse door and leaned it against the wall. "So, where are we going?"

Donna rolled her eyes, trying to keep her rising sense of panic in check. "*I* am going to see…a family friend. Whatever *you're* doing, I hope you have fun."

She watched Navin's expressive face as he battled with varying degrees of disappointment, curiosity, and anger. She wondered which would win. She would never get used to lying to Navin, even though she'd had to do it for most of the time they'd known each other. And she mostly lied by omission, which she liked to think didn't count. Even though she knew it did.

All this because the Order of the Dragon was so strict with her. Still a minor, she had no standing among the alchemists except for being the daughter of two of their legends and the niece of a currently rising star within their ranks. Thinking of Aunt Paige now, Donna couldn't help wondering what she would say if she knew what her charge was considering. How close she finally was to telling Navin the truth.

At least, *some* of the truth. Would that hurt so much?

She could answer that question for herself: of *course* it would hurt. That was why she'd protected him all this time, why she was willing to go along with the secrecy of the Order despite the lies. Navin was blessed with a pretty normal life. It wasn't without its own loss and sadness, but at least his sadness had a human flavor. Donna wanted to protect that normality as much as she could. The thought of Navin suffering the same nightmares that she did filled her with more horror than she could contemplate.

"What is this place?" he asked now, looking around.

"Oh, Navin…why did you have to follow me?" Donna's voice was almost a whisper, but she knew that he'd heard.

His cheeks flushed. "I thought that maybe you were going to meet that guy. Zod, or whatever he's called."

"It's *Xan*, which you totally know. Idiot."

"Hey, you don't know him at all. And you were so spooked last night, outside the house…I was worried about you."

Donna wanted to believe him; she really wanted to believe that Navin had done this out of innocent concern for her. But given the twitchy look on his face, she knew there was a lot more to it than that. *Crap*. She fixed him with a fierce stare and made a decision. "Wait here for a minute."

"But—"

"I said, *wait*." The iron in her voice was a match for the iron that encased her arms. Donna still didn't know how much she would tell him, but Navin was here now and she'd have to figure something out. Even if she left and made him come home with her, there was nothing to stop him from going back alone and doing some investigating on his own, interrupting Maker's work. Donna dreaded what would happen then. While the workshop was hidden in plain sight and looked pretty much abandoned, it was also protected by magical wards that warned Maker whenever anyone unfamiliar approached. And even though Navin had probably already tripped the alarm, making caution pointless, being careful was a tough habit to break.

She pushed open the heavy door to the alchemist's workshop. It wasn't unusual for it to be unlocked, which is why Donna was unprepared for the sight that greeted her as she stepped into the dimly lit workroom, Navin close behind her.

"Maker?" Her voice sounded small in the cavernous space.

The room, although generally filled with junk and metal and machinery of all descriptions, usually had a strange sense of order to it, too. Donna was used to seeing piles of tools and scrap metal all over the place, plans and paperwork on the huge desk against the side wall underneath one of the tall windows, and whatever Maker was currently working on in the center of the room.

Today, however, the disorder in the workshop had none of the old man's personal stamp on it. Papers and files were strewn across the floor like oversized confetti; giant sheets of hammered steel, usually piled up against the far wall, had fallen to the floor as though someone had been trying to look behind them; the central workbench had been swept clear of plans that were now on the floor, the paper crumpled and torn. A plate and mug were smashed to pieces nearby.

"Maker!" Donna called, louder this time.

"What is this place?" Navin's voice echoed around the large open space.

"Shh . . . he's not here. This is weird."

A mechanical clacking and chirping suddenly filled the air, and Donna was forced to duck as something flew overhead.

"What was *that*?" Navin hissed, his voice almost cracking.

They both covered their heads and ducked again as the whirring sounds swept above them.

Donna brushed hair out of her eyes and slowly stood up. "It's okay, they're harmless. Just Maker's birds. He doesn't usually let them out of their cage . . ."

The two clockwork birds—the size of very large crows—were made from brass and copper and iron, with bright silver eyes and polished wings that reflected the natural light from the high windows. They arced and swooped all the way up to the workshop's roof, finally settling in the rafters with a click of metallic claws.

Navin's eyes were the widest she'd ever seen them. "This...'Maker' of yours. Who the heck is he, Donna? The Wonderful Wizard of Oz?"

"Something like that," she muttered, trying to step out of his reach.

But Navin placed a cautionary hand on her shoulder. "Wait. I have a bad feeling about this."

Shaking him off, Donna carefully picked her way around the sharp-edged tools and sea of paper on the floor. Looking up again, she saw that one of the windows had a huge crack in it, spider-webbing outwards in a crazy pattern. Her eyes came to rest on Maker's super-advanced wheelchair, overturned and dumped in the far corner. The old man didn't always need the chair to get around—he had built it himself, and it looked like something out of a comic book—but it helped him when his legs grew weak after too much work.

"What happened?" she whispered.

"Whoever you're looking for isn't here, Donna. I think we should leave." Navin sounded as nervous as she felt.

Donna raised her chin. "No, someone broke in. I'm going to check the kitchen and bathroom before we do anything."

"I think we should just go. We could call the police."

"*You* should go, Navin. You don't even belong here."
Donna's voice shook.

"You can't make me do anything, Donna. You're my friend and I think you're in trouble. I'm not leaving you."

Exasperation flooded Donna's chest and she squeezed her hands into fists. He wasn't making this easy. "Nav…"

"Something's not right—even *I* can see that, and I've never set foot in this place before. It feels… wrong. We should call the cops and just get out."

Donna's mouth thinned. She shook her head as she walked toward the rear of the workshop, heading for the small corridor out back.

"You are so stubborn, woman," muttered Navin. He followed her, nervously checking behind them as though expecting someone to creep up on them at any moment.

Donna couldn't blame him. She had the same feeling herself; the back of her neck was gripped by a horrible prickling sensation, and her stomach clenched with a nauseating sensation of vertigo. "Listen," she hissed.

They both stopped at the entrance to the hallway and held their breath.

A slow scraping was coming from somewhere down the hall, a sound like fingernails on a chalkboard, which was then followed by a high-pitched clicking.

They stared at one another. *What is that?* mouthed Navin, eyes huge.

Donna slid her gaze from his, dread blooming in her gut like a black rose. She couldn't be entirely certain, but she had a very strong suspicion that whatever was in there wasn't human. Or animal. She hated that she knew these dark and unnatural things, but sometimes you just can't deny who you are. Taking a deep breath, she pushed down her fears as best she could and stepped into the dark, narrow corridor.

It was short, and only wide enough for Donna and Navin to walk single file. It ended in a blank white wall. There were only two doors, one on each side of them, about halfway down. The kitchen was on the left, the bathroom to the right. When they reached the left-hand door, Donna turned the handle and pushed it open as wide as she could.

Nothing. The kitchen was tiny, with barely enough room for the two of them. There was a steady *drip-drip-drip* from the tap over the sink. Donna tried to shut it off, but the dripping continued. The tiny window, added almost as an afterthought, was filled with thick patterned glass covered by swirling shapes that precluded any view outside. She could just make out that the morning sun seemed tired and thin, now that winter was almost here.

And then, there it was again. *Scrape-scrape-click-click.* Donna and Navin jumped, and Navin tried to push her behind him, but she pushed back. Harder. She stepped out into the corridor and listened at the other door. She knew that the bathroom was almost as small as the kitchen; there was a little more room in there, but not enough space for much more than the toilet, a sink, and an ornate old-fashioned bathtub.

Scrape-scrape-click-click. The sound set Donna's teeth on edge and made her skin crawl.

Navin nudged her, looking as though he was about to speak. She put one gloved finger to her lips and turned back to the door. She bent against it and listened.

The sound had stopped.

Donna yanked down on the brass handle and pushed. She had to remember to use a "normal" amount of strength. If Navin weren't here, she could break it down without too much trouble.

The door was jammed. Or locked. "Help me," she said, pulling Navin over to the door. "Quickly!"

They both leaned their weight against it, pushing and straining. Donna glanced down at the handle again. "It can't be locked, look. No lock or keyhole. It's just jammed. Hurry up and push. Whatever's in there, it's not getting away."

Navin grunted as he pushed high up on the door, bracing himself against the rotting door frame. Donna heaved from below, leaning her weight on the handle as she used her true strength. The next moment, there was a loud crack as the door burst open and she found herself flying into the room after it, Navin close on her heels. A splintered wooden chair almost tripped her up—it must have been what was jamming the door.

Standing on top of the old-fashioned toilet tank and reaching toward the small, half-open window was a creature that Donna now only saw in her nightmares. As a child, she had played a game where she desperately tried to convince herself that they didn't exist. Not *really*. Even then, she knew it wasn't true.

The creature had nut-brown skin mixed with patches of ash. It was vaguely humanoid, but its skin looked like the bark of an old, old tree. Although about the same height as Donna, it was spindly, with arms and legs that were all joints and angles. Its face was narrow and pointed, with hair like thick moss and narrow black eyes that glinted even in the dim light of the room. The thing's body was clothed in lichen and moss, vines twining around its sharp limbs.

What she found most shocking, though, wasn't its presence, but the fact that it wasn't wearing its *elfskin*—it was acting as though it didn't have anything to hide. Then, with a sudden flash of insight, Donna realized that there was too much iron in the room—the creature wasn't able to hold a different shape in here; its glamour was pretty much worthless. That old iron tub was causing it all sorts of problems.

She was only vaguely aware of Navin beside her, breathing heavily and too fast. She felt a stab of sympathy for him as he tried to make sense of the impossibility standing right in front of them.

The creature opened its lipless mouth, a dark slash across its twisted face. Donna's mind flashed back to the shadow she'd seen sliding through the darkness outside Xan's house. She hadn't been imagining things, after all.

The wood elves had returned to the city.

Four

Scrape-scrape-click-click.

The sound kicked Donna out of her trance. She grabbed Navin's arm and pushed him back toward the door. "Get out."

"Donna…"

"Get out!" she yelled.

He backed up a step but didn't leave.

Donna moved slowly toward the creature—the elf—on shaking legs, trying to look braver than she felt. She tried to ignore the sudden, stabbing pains in her wrists.

Nightmarish images crept at the edges of her mind and she tried to block them, not wanting to remember. The smell of wet earth filled her nostrils as she got closer, making it seem all the more real.

"Stay where you are," she said quietly, but with an unmistakable edge of menace. She sensed Navin glance sharply at her, and registered the surprise on his face from the corner of her eye. Damn, he was still in the bathroom. Trying to protect her.

"What are you doing here?" she demanded of the creature. "Where's Maker?" She didn't really expect a reply. At least, not one that she could understand.

A sly look crossed the elf's face—it was a disturbingly human expression. Its feet clung to the ceramic toilet tank like gnarled roots.

And then it sprung at them with no sound or warning, throwing itself forward and using its deceptively strong legs as pistons. Its bony, twiglike fingers latched onto Navin's shoulders and its full weight drove him straight back against the sink. All the air rushed out of Navin in an audible *whoosh*, and he made a strangled cry of pain as his back struck the chunky ceramic basin.

Donna, knocked off balance, scrambled to regain her footing. She looked frantically around for some kind of weapon. Her eyes fell on a sink plunger, and she made a grab for it. Navin was trying to pry the elf's clawed hands off his jacket, but the thing was stronger, hanging on and making that inhuman clicking sound at the back of its throat. Its jaws opened to reveal a mouthful of needle-sharp, yellow teeth. It tried to reach Navin's terrified face with them.

With a shout of rage, Donna began hitting the elf over the back of the head with the wooden end of the plunger. "Get off him!"

The thing hissed and turned toward her, keeping one hand attached to Navin. It tried to bat the improvised weapon from her shaking hands, but she had a death-grip on it. A sudden idea came to her and she reversed the plunger, brandishing the suction end at the elf. Yeah, she thought, like this is gonna work.

Navin, who was still trying to pull the elf's claws off his jacket, throwing in a few hard kicks at its spindly legs for good measure, suddenly appeared to have an idea of his own; Donna caught the flash in his wide brown eyes and knew he was up to something. With a twist of his shoulders and a violent heave, he shrugged himself free of his jacket and threw himself out of the way.

Now he was free and the creature was left holding the biker jacket. With a look of almost-human disgust on its creased face, it threw the jacket to the ground. Donna used its surprise to her advantage and, feeling only slightly ridiculous, shoved the sink plunger straight into its face, smiling grimly when she heard the satisfying sound of the suction taking hold. She used all her strength, ignoring the stabbing pain in her hands, and swung the creature around with its face stuck firmly to the plunger. Its arms flailed as it tried to grab onto something, but it could do nothing as Donna—almost high on adrenaline—flung it in the direction of the tub.

The plunger came free with a loud *pop* and the elf flew into the tub, crashing over the side and landing inside with an inhuman shriek. Smoke immediately began to rise from its earthen flesh, and it screamed as it tried to scramble over the deep sides of the tub.

The bathroom was filled with the smell of burning, like wood-smoke. Donna pushed Navin toward the door. "Let's go, come on. Out!"

Navin seemed frozen, looking from Donna to the bathtub with a shocked expression, but she didn't have time to worry about that right now. "Please, Navin, move!" She shoved him again.

"Wait," he said. "My jacket."

"Forget it. Run!"

Navin dodged around Donna and snatched the jacket from the floor. "*Now* we can go."

The injured creature, meanwhile, had managed to scramble out of the tub and seemed undecided whether to make another grab for its prey or escape while it still could. Smoke swept through the room, despite the partly opened window. Backing toward the door, Donna threw the plunger as the thing hissed and turned away, watching them with its head ducked down low, alternately sneering and cringing.

"Navin, come *on*!"

They bolted from the room. As Donna pulled the door closed, she caught a final glimpse of their attacker, leaping toward the window.

"It's going to get away," she said. "Maybe we can cut it off round the back."

Navin gripped her arm. "What do you mean, 'maybe we can cut it off'? Are you *crazy*? That thing tried to *bite* me. I'm not giving it another chance to take a chunk out of my face."

Donna felt shock waves of adrenaline in her chest, making it difficult to breathe. "You're right, sorry. I got carried away."

Navin's face had visibly paled and his pupils were huge, making his normally soft brown eyes look almost completely black. "You think?" His voice cracked.

Taking a deep breath, Donna tried to think calm thoughts. "Are you okay, Navin?" She knew how ridiculous it must sound even as the words left her mouth.

Navin still looked shell-shocked. "What was that...that *monster*?"

Something inside Donna crumbled. What was she supposed to tell him? How could she ever look Navin in the eyes again? After everything they'd been through together over the last few years—his mother's death, which had been just awful, and her getting kicked out of school, which hadn't exactly been a cakewalk—now she had to deal with telling him the truth. Her worst fears were materializing, and there wasn't a damn thing she could do about it. There was no rewind button on real life, much as she might wish otherwise. This wasn't like the many movies they'd watched together, curled up in either Nav's bedroom or hers, shutting out the world and losing themselves in fantasy.

She took a deep breath. "That was a wood elf ... or, a dark elf. They get called that more, these days. It makes it easier for the Order to justify hunting them."

"What's the Order? And ... Donna, are you seriously telling me that was an *elf*?"

Donna nodded gravely. "Yes. Aunt Paige says—"

"Your *aunt*? What the *hell* is going on, Donna?"

She slumped against the wall, breathing in the dusty air of the narrow corridor and scrubbing a gloved hand wearily across her face. "Look, I know this is a lot to take in. But it's not like you don't already know there are strange things about me. About my life. I mean, I know I haven't told you about those things, but ... Nav, you're not stupid. You told me yourself you'd followed me here because of all the so-called secrets I've been keeping from you." She clamped down on the thought that maybe he'd only followed her because he'd been jealous of Xan. That was way more than she could handle right now.

Navin ran a frustrated hand through his messed-up hair, holding his jacket almost protectively against his chest with the other hand. "Yeah, but I didn't expect it to be *this*. I mean, having a paranoid aunt is one thing, but...*elves*? Come on, Donna. There's weird, and then there's completely bat-shit crazy."

"We can't talk about this now; we need to get out of here."

Navin continued as though she hadn't spoken. "And you were fighting it like you knew what you were doing. What's *that* about?"

Donna gave a snort of laughter. "Yeah, sure, I *really* knew what I was doing. Sink Plunger Girl."

"Well, you knew a whole lot more than me." He glared at her, an unfamiliar tightness in his jaw, and then headed back into the workshop.

"Don't be mad at me, Nav. Please, I can't stand it."

He sighed. "I'm not mad. I'm just...scared, I guess."

Throughout their awkward conversation, Donna had been casting fearful glances around them, half-expecting the elf to appear again although it was probably long gone. She shuddered as she remembered the sound it made, and its dark eyes. She wondered if she would ever be able to shake the image of its razorlike teeth straining toward Navin's face.

She shook her head and tried to focus on what Navin was saying.

"Who is this Maker dude, anyway?" He was shrugging himself back into his jacket, and Donna was relieved to see that some of the color had returned to his cheeks. "Do you think that thing had something to do with him not being here?"

"I don't know." Donna hated feeling so uncertain. She tried to think what to do next. Tell Aunt Paige? Or go straight to Quentin? Something had happened to Maker, and her first move should be to report his disappearance to Quentin Frost, the Order's archmaster—their "leader" for as long as she could remember. Not to mention report the current state of his workshop, and the fact that there'd been a wood elf hiding out in the bathroom.

"Donna, you're not *telling* me anything," Navin said, the frustration clear in his voice. "Help me out here."

She sighed. "I'll tell you more at home."

He fixed her with determined eyes. "You promise? You'll tell me *everything*?"

Donna squeezed her fingers open and shut, wondering how much Navin could really take. "Everything" would be a lot for even the most open-minded person. "I'll try, Nav. That's all I can promise you."

It would have to be enough for now, and she turned her back on Navin before he could say anything else. What was she going to do? All these years of secrecy, and now the lid had well and truly been ripped off of Pandora's Box. She didn't think Navin would let her put the lid back on any time soon, and she trembled at the thought of the consequences if she started spilling the Order's secrets.

Donna wasn't even thinking about the potential consequences for herself; she was far more worried about what it could mean for Navin. He was an innocent. (Quentin would call him a "commoner," an archaic term that she hated.) But how could Navin Sharma really be considered innocent after coming face-to-face with a dark elf?

Not even the alchemists could wipe someone's memory. At least, she didn't think they could.

As she walked away from the building, Donna took grateful gulps of cold air. What mattered was that Navin was safe. He had his back to her as he fiddled with his bike, which he'd left by the door. She felt like crying, but knew that wouldn't help things. Her duty was to the Order—to her aunt. That had to come first.

The door to the workshop, which they'd been careful to close, suddenly banged opened. Navin almost got crushed behind it, and Donna's heart began racing so hard she felt dizzy.

Maker stood in the doorway, blinking in the brightening sun.

"Maker!" Donna ran toward him. "You're okay!"

"Okay" was probably something of an overstatement. The old alchemist was leaning on his walking stick and looking frail. The fact that he wasn't in his wheelchair was usually a good sign—it meant he had strength in his legs that day—but there was no denying how pale and drawn his lined face was. And Donna had already seen his wheelchair, tossed aside like nothing more than scrap metal. The sudden image made her mouth go dry.

"What are you doing here, child?" Maker's voice was hoarse. He doubled over into a coughing fit.

Distressed, Donna wondered what she should do to help. Theirs was not a demonstrative relationship. She'd known Maker all her life and seen him frequently over the last ten years, thanks to the work he did on her hands and arms, but he wasn't exactly huggable. She touched his arm tentatively.

As her hand made contact with the dark flannel of his work shirt, she felt a burning heat radiating from his body. Even through her gloves. Pain shot toward her wrist.

"Maker, I don't think you're well. Here, let me help you." She shot Navin a glance she hoped he understood. Her friend was hovering nearby, having squeezed out from behind the heavy door, and looked as though he might try to take the old man's other arm. Not a good idea.

Maybe Maker was just tired, but there was a quality of strain about him that Donna wasn't used to seeing. She could smell a sharp-edged sourness; it reminded her of the stale scent of water that had held flowers for too long.

"Donna, please stop fussing. I'm fine." Maker brushed her away with his free hand. And yet the fine sheen of sweat on his brow and the crease between his eyebrows told her that things were very far from fine. He took a breath and appeared to make an effort to steady himself. "Really, I'm quite well."

She bit her lip. "Is it safe to go back inside?"

He nodded briskly. "Yes, yes. Everything has been dealt with."

"You mean, you…" Donna let her voice trail off, wondering what Maker had done to "deal with" the wood elf. Last she'd seen, it was attempting to escape from the bathroom window. And the alchemist hadn't been anywhere around at the time; she was sure of it.

"The creature has been neutralized. It was just a stray." Maker's wintry blue eyes focused on Navin and narrowed.

Donna cringed. How was she going to explain his presence? This was a breach of confidence that would surely be unforgivable.

"Aren't you going to introduce me to your friend, Donna?"

Navin stepped forward and Donna reached down for his hand. She gave it a gentle squeeze. "This is Navin Sharma. Navin, this is Maker. He…works with my aunt." She took a deep breath. "Maker, I'm sorry about Nav being here. It won't happen again—it was a mistake."

Maker's expression softened. "I think we can come to some kind of agreement, don't you?"

"Agreement?" Donna frowned.

"I don't want Paige worrying about you and what happened here." He nodded in the direction of his workshop. "Normally my experiments don't run away before I've finished with them."

Experiments? Donna's stomach clenched. That didn't sound right. Since when did the alchemists experiment on stray elves?

Before she could interject, Maker continued. "If you take your friend away and promise that he will never return"—here he gave Navin a fierce look—"we will say nothing more about this. *Any* of it. Do you understand? I don't want to share my findings with Simon until I'm sure of something."

Simon? Simon Gaunt? He was Quentin Frost's partner—they'd been a couple for many years, at least for as long as Donna had known them—and he was also the official secretary of the Order, Quentin's right-hand man. Simon Gaunt gave her the creeps, if she was honest about it, and it made Donna go cold to think there were secrets between him and Maker.

She wasn't exactly sure what was going on, but it seemed like Maker was willing to let the Navin situation go, so long as she didn't tell about the wood elf in the workshop. At least, for now. It was a deal she could live with.

Except that something definitely wasn't right. Where had Maker come from? She'd been all over the workshop and the corridor out back, and there'd been no sign of him. Had he seen them come in? Also, it really was strange that Maker wasn't angrier about Navin, since secrets were a fact of life for the Order. Then again, seeing how Maker was being oh-so-reasonable about Nav's presence, it could be an unexpected gift. Maybe she shouldn't be in such a hurry to risk messing with that.

And of course, if she ignored Maker's request and told Aunt Paige what had happened, what if she ended up getting everything wrong? Donna didn't want to look like she'd been sneaking around, or worse, let on that she suspected something horrible had been happening in Maker's workshop. Especially when he'd never given her reason to think badly of him before. Just the thought of telling Aunt Paige that Navin had encountered an elf made her feel sick. There could be no going back from that—not for her, and certainly not for Navin.

She watched as a bead of sweat slipped slowly down the side of Maker's face. He must be exhausted after handling the dark elf all by himself, despite the magic Donna knew he could craft. Alchemy—*real* magic—was all about transformation. It was a very different sort of power than the ridiculous things that regular people saw in movies. You didn't just wave a wand and say a few words; there was a lot of work involved. Painstaking preparation and ritual. Maker always said "magic is technology," and Donna hadn't fully understood this until the first time she saw his workshop.

Pulling herself upright, she smiled tightly at the old alchemist. "We'll get out of your way, then. Don't worry, I won't breathe a word—and neither will Navin." She raised her eyebrows at him. "Will you?"

Navin had been watching this exchange while slouching against the wall with his arms crossed. He was doing his best impression of Harmless and Totally Trustworthy.

Donna almost smiled despite the tension in the air. He was a terrible actor.

"Huh?" he replied.

"Nav, I said you'll keep your mouth shut about all of this. Right?"

"Right," he agreed, nodding so hard she thought he'd lost control of his neck muscles. "I won't say a word. Never. I'll take it to my grave and—"

"Nav?" Donna cut in.

"What?"

"Shut up."

"Shutting up." He made a zipping motion across his lips, mimed twisting a lock shut, and threw the imaginary key over his shoulder.

Rolling her eyes, Donna wished she could avoid telling him all the things she'd been forced to keep from him for so long. The truth was a slippery slope, and once it was really *out there*, it would be impossible to stop it from taking on a life of its own. While she didn't generally believe in the power of prayer—she'd given up on all that when her father died and her mother got sick—right now she would try just about anything. Swallowing past the sudden dryness in her throat, Donna prayed that revealing her secrets wouldn't be the biggest mistake of her life.

She prayed that Navin wouldn't turn his back on her, once he knew the whole dark and twisted truth.

Five

D onna sat cross-legged on her bed as Navin slouched (his usual position) into the oversized beanbag on her bedroom floor. They had done this for the last three years—talking far into the night in either her room or his, whether or not there was school the next day.

"So," said Navin.

"So."

"Elves." He raised an eyebrow.

"Uh-huh."

"It didn't look much like Orlando Bloom…"

Donna threw the nearest cushion at his head. "I wondered how long it would take you."

"What?" He gave her his best wounded expression, all big brown eyes and indignation.

She forced a smile, trying to push down a rising sense of panic. She was so tired thinking about it all; why couldn't she just have a normal life?

"Earth to Donna," Navin said.

"Sorry. I was just…you know. Thinking."

Navin heaved himself out of the beanbag chair and came over to sit on the bed next to her. He put his arm around her and she gratefully leaned into his warmth, her head resting on his shoulder.

"Donna, it'll be okay. Whatever it is, you can tell me."

"Navin, it's not that simple…"

"So make it simple. Just tell me what that thing was— what this *means*."

"It's just that I'm not supposed to tell. *Anyone*. Not even you."

"I'm not going to say anything. Who am I going to tell? Dad? Nisha? She'd open her big mouth to her friends if I told her what color your bedroom walls are, never mind any of this stuff."

Donna bit back a smile. Navin's younger sister wasn't known for her discretion. "She's just young."

"She's fifteen and should know better by now. She's such a little gossip." Navin shifted on the bed and Donna lifted her eyes to his. "Anyway, forget her. Tell me about that thing back at Maker's. The...elf. And who *is* this Maker? Is that his real name?"

"I think we should start with him—and with the Order. You need to know that before you can understand the more crazy stuff."

Navin nodded, for all the world as if there was anything sane about any of this. "Right. The Order. You mentioned it back at the workshop. Is it, like, something to do with witchcraft? A group your aunt belongs to?"

Donna sighed. Here went nothing. "Yes, it is a group Aunt Paige belongs to—a group she was born into, just like I was—but it's got nothing to do with witchcraft or paganism. It's actually short for 'The Order of the Dragon.' The members are alchemists, and it's a secret society that's been around for centuries."

"Please don't tell me there are actual dragons involved." There was a pained expression on Navin's face. "I'm trying to be cool here, but that might ruin everything."

Donna couldn't hold back a smile. "Don't worry, it's just a symbolic thing. There are four alchemical Orders, but ours is the oldest and one of the only ones that's still actively involved in anything magical. The dragon has always been linked with alchemy, especially the great serpent, the ouroboros. It's usually shown lying in a circle—mouth to tail—devouring itself."

"Magic?" Navin said faintly. "For real? Is it like in *Charmed*? Because I think I could handle that. Maybe."

Donna knew that the only reason Navin watched *Charmed* was because of his huge crush on Alyssa Milano. "Are you listening to any of this?" she demanded. "You're the one who insisted on knowing the truth." She was trying to hide how afraid she was that every word out of her mouth would drive Navin further and further away.

"I'm listening. I'm fine." The expression on Navin's face said that he was anything *but* fine, despite his enthusiasm for her blowing away his entire worldview. "What were you saying about... um... Oberon?"

"*Ouroboros*. It's a symbol. Here, let me show you." Donna swung her legs off the bed and crouched down by her bookshelves, glad of an excuse to move. To *do* something. Grabbing a thick volume jacketed in a glossy collection of symbols from around the world, she flopped back down next to Navin and began leafing through the heavily illustrated pages. She jabbed her finger at what looked like an ancient bronze seal. It was stamped with the image of a simple yet highly stylized serpent, curled in a circle with its mouth and tail almost indistinguishable.

"See? It has different names depending on the culture, but the most important thing is what it symbolizes. It's something to do with 'all being One,' and it reminds us that the cycle of death and rebirth might be considered a natural thing. Although death is something that alchemy seeks to overcome."

The part of the mythology she didn't tell Navin was the part she'd held close to her heart ever since her father's death. In traditional alchemy, it was only by symbolically "slaying the dragon" that any kind of real transformation could occur. Donna knew that she had a long way to go before she was ready to face her *own* personal dragon—the monster that had destroyed everything good in her life— but the belief that she would someday face it had kept her going through many painfully long nights.

Navin was looking thoughtful as he stared at the image of the ouroboros, and she knew that he must be thinking of his own loss. His mother's illness and passing had been hard on all the Sharmas, but Donna knew that Navin still mourned her every single day. They'd talked, before, about how his family's Hinduism had helped his father to cope; back then, Donna had had to fake the whole pagan thing when they were comparing experiences. She wondered how Navin would react to the ideas she had *really* been brought up with—alchemy wasn't exactly an easy subject to come to terms with, and it was more science than religion despite what many detractors would say to the contrary.

"Okay," Navin said. "So I get it. Alchemy, life and death, blah blah blah. What else? Tell me about the other three Orders—you said there are four."

Donna slammed the book shut and dumped it on the floor. She crossed her legs on the bed and began counting on her fingers: "The Order of the Crow, the Order of the Lion, and the Order of the Rose."

He frowned. "Rose?"

"What's so funny about that?"

"Well, there are three Orders that are all, *rah*, scary creatures; and then there's the 'Order of the Rose.' Sounds kinda lame to me."

Donna rolled her eyes. "That's because you don't understand Hermeticism."

"Hermeti-*what*?"

"Never mind. Just go with it: Dragon, Crow, Lion, and Rose. That's the way it's always been. And like I said, the others aren't so important these days. Well, apart from the Order of the Crow. We have what some old-school practitioners call Dragon Magic, and they have their Crow Magic in England. But each Order is very different and follows a separate mission. We don't see representatives from the other Orders very often—like, once a year is pretty much it."

Navin smirked. "At the annual Alchemy Con?"

"This is *serious*." Donna swatted him with the cushion she'd been leaning against.

Deflecting the blow with ease and grabbing another pillow, Navin pretended to suffocate her with it. "And this is my way of dealing with it."

She pushed him away impatiently, though she could hardly blame him. "Okay, so that's the Order—"

"Hold on a second there, Underwood, we haven't even scratched the surface yet."

"Nav, there isn't time to give you every single detail. I've been a part of this my whole life; it would take forever!"

His face was serious again. "I know that. But what do alchemists *do*? Surely they're not really searching for the philosopher's stone? Even I've heard of those myths, but... is that real?"

Donna wrapped her arms around herself and leaned against the wall. She couldn't tell him everything; she just couldn't bring herself to talk about the Order's hunger for eternal life and their single-minded dedication to that cause. Especially not after the whole wood-elf-in-the-workshop incident—it made her feel nauseous to even think about it. She needed to figure some things out before she could even consider going there.

"Well?" Navin nudged her with his knee.

"It's complicated, but for one thing, there's the science of it all—which would include things like the philosopher's stone and the elixir of life." She saw that Navin was about to say something and rushed on. "Transformation. That's a huge area of study and practice, way too huge to go into now. If you've read any kind of fiction about alchemy, heard the legends, or seen it in a movie...you at least get the idea. Maker's a very powerful alchemist. He makes things—as his name suggests."

Navin screwed up his face. "Like, what things?"

She blew out a breath. "Just...stuff. Lots and lots of different kinds of stuff."

"Magical stuff?"

"Sometimes, yes. You saw some of it at his workshop." She curled her legs beneath her and fixed him with a determined stare, one that dared him to interrupt her again. "And then there are the elves."

"So, you're skipping over the part where you guys make gold," Navin said dryly, "and I get to hear about the monsters. Great."

Ignoring him, Donna continued, wondering if this was how her tutor, Alma Kensington, felt after all those years of teaching her. She already felt exhausted, and Navin had only known about the magical reality of her life for a few hours. "So, the creature we ran into today was a wood elf, although the Order also calls them dark elves since they're among the most dangerous beings to come out of Faerie."

Navin leaned forward. "'Faerie'?"

"Oh, right. Sorry, I mean the place. That's what it's called."

"You're seriously telling me there's a place called *Faerie*."

Donna wasn't sure if Navin meant this as a question or a statement. "Um, yeah. It's another realm that exists right alongside ours." She caught the look on his face. "What? You thought our world is all there is? That's so...limited."

"Well, excuse me for being *limited*."

"As I was saying," Donna said loudly, talking over him, "when the faeries—as in, the actual *beings*—left this world and finally went back to their own realm, the wood elves got left behind. They refused to pay the tithe, you see—"

"Wait a minute. Tithe?"

"The tithe that Faerie has to pay to Hell every seven years."

"*Hell*?!"

Donna grabbed his arm, for a moment forgetting her own strength. "Keep your voice down," she hissed. "I don't know when Aunt Paige will get back."

"Shit, chill *out*." Navin's brown eyes were filled with reproach. "I bruise easily." He rubbed his arm and wouldn't quite look at her.

Donna threw her arms round his shoulders—taking more care this time—and hugged him. "I'm sorry; she just can't find out I've told you all this. Ever."

"It's okay, Underwood. I get it." His arms went around her in return, and he stroked her back before gently pushing her away.

Donna cleared her throat and decided it might just be easier to keep talking. This was getting way too intense. "It's not like the Christian place. Hell's just a convenient name for the demon realm—the Underworld. The tithe is like a payment. A penalty of sorts. If they don't pay it…well, I don't really know what happens. But the wood elves refused to pay their tithe to the demons, and war broke out between them and the rest of the fey—resulting in the elves being left behind in the human world. They got all evil and twisted, the longer they had to stay here."

She shrugged, trying to remember the things she'd learned from Alma over the years. According to alchemical lore, there were three main races, or factions—humans, protected by the alchemists; the fey, of which the wood elves were just one subculture; and the demons, which Donna knew next to nothing about and would be entirely happy to remain ignorant of for the rest of her life. She gazed at Navin, waiting for him to say something.

He finally spoke. "If they're *wood* elves, where do they live? There's not much of the old Ironwood left now—it's not even really a forest at all, is it?"

"No, and even what's left is under threat. If the Order had its way, it would've been pulled down and built over long ago. But environmental do-gooders have managed to block that, so far." Although the Ironwood was still a protected area, Donna knew that the Order hadn't given up. Aunt Paige was working quietly through her position in the mayor's office, and the Order was making the case—through various politicians—that much-needed housing should be built on the site.

Navin looked thoughtful. "I was always on the side of those do-gooders…"

"Yeah, well, now you know what's out there." Donna picked at a loose thread on the purple throw they were sitting on.

"So, they live out there in what's left of the woods? That's—"

"Crazy?"

He laughed, but it came out sounding strained. "I guess." He leaned back against the wall and scrubbed at his face with his hands. "But then, this whole thing is crazy."

Donna nodded sympathetically, trying to hide her growing trepidation. She couldn't help it; she was analyzing every move Navin made, looking for signs that this was all too much for him. That she was going to lose him. So far he seemed to be taking things pretty well—maybe *too* well.

"Anyway," she continued, "the wood elves got left behind, so, yes, they mainly stayed in the forests and woodland. But then the progress of humans began to push them out of their natural habitat."

"Of course." Navin nodded. "Tearing down forests, building over them, that sort of thing."

"The Iron Age," Donna said darkly. "Ironbridge has expanded so much over the years—from village to town, and then to the small city it is today. Think of the land it encompasses now, compared to what it used to cover. Some people are actually living on top of what used to be a settlement belonging to faeries. At one time, the woodland extended much farther; that's why the iron bridge was built in the first place, back when this was only a village. It was supposed to keep the elves out. We're living over the center of the old Elflands."

"Man, I bet they were pissed off about losing their home."

"And losing it more than once. First they get kicked out of Faerie—their own realm, then they start getting uprooted from their natural environment in the human world."

Navin suddenly looked worried. "So what's to stop them from overrunning the place, like that one in Maker's workshop?"

Donna shook her head. "You saw what happened to it when it fell in the tub. They can't stand being near iron—not for too long, anyway. And it always hurts them to come into actual contact with it. They get sort of thin and stretched; their magic doesn't work properly. Of course…"

The look of relief that had momentarily crossed Navin's face was wiped away. "What?"

"Well, they've adapted, to some extent. Among all the beings of Faerie, the dark elves have a unique kind of magic. They're shape-changers."

"Great, now they can 'walk among us.'" Navin made spooky *Twilight Zone* sounds.

Donna glared at him. "They really can. They can change their shape and wear another form. It's called their 'elfskin.' It's like the ultimate disguise."

"How do we know they're not taking over Ironbridge, then?"

"Because the Order has magic of its own that can find them. Sniff out the ones who *do* try to come here. And don't forget the iron—cities are half built of the stuff.

Even wearing a glamour, elves couldn't survive here. Sure, they might be able to withstand the iron for a while, but not for any length of time, and not unless they have some additional source of power."

"So, let me get this straight. The alchemists—these four Orders—basically make it their business to...what? Fight the elves? All faeries? What's the deal?"

"I guess, historically, the alchemists were always the ones who stood between humanity and the fey—as in, anything that comes out of Faerie. But in modern times, it's very different. The dark elves are the only threat now, because they're the only ones who have any sort of major presence. And even *their* numbers are shrinking."

Of course, there were also faery stragglers, solitary fey who had gotten left behind or who had chosen not to go with their people when Faerie was sealed up for good. Not to mention changelings and half-fey. But Donna didn't think now was the time to mention this. She'd probably already taken a few years off Navin's life just telling him as much as she had.

Navin uncurled his legs and stretched. "So, assuming I'm going to believe all of this—which I do, don't worry— when are you going to tell me about *these*?" He suddenly laid his brown hand over hers. Her gloves had always been a barrier between them. "Don't you think it's way past time?"

Donna pulled her hand back. It was a reflexive action, but the moment she'd done it, she wished she could undo it. The hurt and rejection on his face made her heart ache. "Nav, I—"

"Donna!" called a voice from downstairs, "I'm home!"

Saved by Aunt Paige, Donna thought. Who'd've thunk it? For the past year, she'd managed to avoid telling Navin the truth behind the Incident at Ironbridge High, and she figured her luck had finally run out. But it hadn't.

"Up here with Nav, Aunt Paige," she shouted back. She turned to Navin, trying to tell him how sorry she was with her eyes. "I should go talk to her. I've hardly seen her since she got back from her trip."

"What are you going to tell her?"

"Maker said not to say anything." Donna shrugged, trying to ignore the doubt that tightened her gut. "I guess he must know what he's doing." Something was off about that whole situation, but she had too much to sort through right now.

Navin got up and waited for her to follow him to the bedroom door, but Donna couldn't help noticing that he wasn't looking at her. "Come on then, let me go say 'hi' to your aunt so I can get home," he said. "Dad'll wonder what's happened to me."

They stood there for a moment, Donna wishing she knew what was going through her best friend's mind. It was a pity that being a child of alchemists didn't give her special powers—like telepathy, or cool stuff like that.

Navin's face was paler than normal now, and there were little patches of putty-colored skin beneath his eyes that looked strange against his light brown skin. It sometimes happened when he got tired or stressed; Donna had seen him like this during exams, and especially around the time of his mother's illness. Guilt made her chest tight and she found it difficult to breathe. *She* had made him look like that. It was her fault that Nav was so shell-shocked.

And betrayed, said the guilt-ridden voice inside her.

As usual, Navin surprised her. He grabbed her hand and gave it a quick squeeze. "Don't look so worried, Underwood."

"I'm so sorry about all of this," she replied, unable to stop her voice from wobbling and immediately hating herself for sounding weak. "If anything ever happened to you, it would be my fault."

"Stop with the drama." He let go of her hand and flung his arm around her shoulders. "Women! Always exaggerating."

She snorted. "Sharma, you know just what to say to say to a girl. No wonder you haven't hooked up with anyone yet."

"Who says I haven't?"

"I'd know if you had." Donna tried to smile as she stepped away from him. "You tell me everything."

The words were out of her mouth before she could stop them.

Navin looked at her carefully. She had never seen him look more solemn. All the humor drained out of him, and his mouth, usually so quick to smile, had drawn into a tight line. "Maybe I don't tell you everything, Don. We all have secrets. I just learned that today."

She bit her lip. Dammit, this was something she would not be able to stand; there was no way she could go on without Navin beside her. But he was right. She *had* kept secrets; maybe too many of them for their friendship to survive. She had always believed that she didn't have a choice—the Order had its rules, and she'd followed them because…well, because that's what you do when you grow up among the alchemists.

But of course, now she knew an important but painful truth: the choice had been hers all along. Donna had *chosen* to follow the rules.

That choice could cost her the most important person in her life; it could cost her Navin.

Six

After Navin had gone, Donna lay on her bed listening to the familiar sounds of her aunt clattering mugs and plates in the kitchen. She reluctantly contemplated putting in an appearance for tea, not really wanting to face her aunt while she was still so confused about everything.

She was supposed to be doing homework, but there wasn't a chance she'd be able to concentrate on Hermetic Literature with everything that had happened since last night. Swallowing hard, she tried to think about something else, something comforting and normal.

The fact that Aunt Paige was making afternoon tea seemed ridiculously mundane in light of recent developments. They usually spent some time catching up on Sundays—time that didn't have anything to do with either Donna's education and training or her aunt's work. Paige was very busy during the week and often away on Saturdays, meaning that Sunday was the one day they really got to spend quality time together.

Donna's mind wandered back to the conversation with Navin. Not only had she broken one of the Order's most sacred vows, but she'd involved her friend way more than was safe. She'd pretty much spilled her guts and told him everything. Okay, maybe not everything, but a *lot*. She still hadn't shown him her hands and arms, but no doubt that would be next.

She remembered the carefully controlled expressions of shock on Navin's face while he listened to her, and the way he'd looked at her before he left. The disappointment and the worry—and the darkness in his eyes that said he almost didn't recognize her—would stay with her forever. That look, especially, was completely her fault. Just as she'd been allowing herself to believe it might be okay, that Navin was handling things well, she'd pulled away from his touch. He had finally asked her about her hands—something he'd never pressed her about—and she'd shrunk from him.

Some friend I am, she thought.

Her phone beeped and she grabbed it from the bedside table. She hoped it meant Navin was okay and not going completely nuts just thinking about all the things she'd told him. But the number on the display was unfamiliar. Donna frowned. It wasn't like many people sent her text messages.

Holding her breath, and suddenly getting a clear mental image of intense green eyes, she read the message several times before she could fully take it in:

Please meet me for coffee. We need to talk. X

For one crazy moment, Donna thought the message had been signed with a kiss. Then she remembered that "X" was Xan's initial. *Duh.*

She bit her lip and tried not to get too excited. Or too nervous. So he wanted to meet—it didn't mean anything. It wasn't like it was a date. Her hands felt clumsy as she fiddled with the phone and wondered what she should say in reply. Then she smiled and began to type.

I thought you were going to CALL me? I call this texting ;-)

The reply came back within seconds:

I find it easier to take rejection in writing...

Her grin widened and she couldn't stop a delicious, warm feeling from bubbling up inside her. Her heart felt lighter and, for the first time that day, the shadow of worry began to melt into the background.

They texted back and forth, arranging a meeting at the center of Ironbridge Common at four thirty the next day, which was the earliest Donna thought she could make it after her classes with Alma Kensington. She wouldn't even have to tell Aunt Paige where she was going, since she often met Navin after school and rarely went straight home from the Frost Estate.

Staring at her cell phone, Donna wondered how she was going to be able to concentrate between now and then.

"Donna!" Aunt Paige called. "I thought you were coming downstairs. I've made the tea…"

Donna jumped guiltily off the bed. "Coming!"

She was suddenly nervous about spending time with her aunt; she'd never been good at hiding things from her. She tried to put all thoughts of Xan and Navin, and especially Maker, out of her mind. But… she felt sure the old alchemist was up to something. The most disturbing thing about all of it was that Maker hadn't even seemed phased about hiding a dark elf in his workshop. It was almost as though it had been *normal*. And the word "experiment" set all sorts of alarm bells ringing.

Shaking her head, Donna shoved her feet into fluffy slippers and ran downstairs to see her aunt.

"Tonight?" Donna gasped.

Aunt Paige pursed her lips and ran a hand through her dark hair. "It's only once a month. I don't think I ask much of you, Donna." She was using the no-nonsense tone that was an all too familiar feature of her strong personality.

"I really can't go, not tonight." The monthly dinners with the alchemists were something Donna was resenting more and more with each passing year. It was like being indoctrinated into something. If there was one thing she hated above all else, it was not being given a *choice*—a regular feature of the life she'd been born into.

Aunt Paige held her gaze, glancing away only to fold up the cuffs of her soft red sweater. Her casual clothes today made her look only slightly less intimidating; a tall woman, Paige Underwood usually lived in fitted charcoal trouser-suits. She was Donna's father's sister, three years younger than him, and was very well regarded among the alchemists. The Order had thrown a big party for her on her fortieth birthday, with a dizzying array of members from other Orders in attendance. Quentin Frost had turned his estate into the perfect high-class venue: there had been a marquee, beautiful catering, and even a live band.

Of course, Donna would rather have celebrated her aunt's birthday in a quieter way, but Quentin wouldn't hear of it. Not for one of the Order's "Moon Sisters"—an ancient name for female alchemists that Donna had always found amusing. Apparently it was a title she herself could look forward to if she followed in her parents' footsteps and became a full initiate when she was eighteen. It wasn't something she liked to think about, because it wasn't something she wanted to *do*. She just hadn't gotten around to telling anybody that. And she wasn't entirely sure that they would even listen to her if she did.

Aunt Paige's face was lined with tension, as always. She worked full-time in the offices of the Mayor of Ironbridge, and by all accounts he was a hard taskmaster. But Paige thrived on the workload, and Donna knew that the real reason she worked there was so she could keep the Order informed of any relevant insider political information. It wasn't unusual for alchemists to be situated in high places; centuries ago, in countries like Great Britain, it was thought that some alchemists were royal spies.

When Donna didn't offer any further information, Aunt Paige crossed her arms. "And why is it that you can't come with me tonight? Do you have plans with Navin?" The unspoken word "again" hung in the air between them.

"No, it's just that…" Donna swallowed and stirred her tea. "I was planning to visit Mom this evening." Okay, so it was an excuse, but she really *should* go see her mother. It was long past time.

Her aunt's tone softened. "Really? That's wonderful news—she'll be so happy to see you."

Donna doubted that. For the most part, Rachel Underwood didn't recognize her own daughter when Donna visited her at the exclusive and very private Institute. The residents were mainly elderly, but there were a handful of younger patients, her mother among them. Nobody quite knew what to do with her—she wasn't exactly crazy, but she certainly wasn't … *well*. It was more like there was a void where once a person had existed. A beautiful, vibrant person, who was now an empty shell who rarely spoke.

All of that vitality, snuffed out after one night of terror in the forest.

"Well," Donna said, "I haven't been for weeks."

"All the more reason to go, then."

Aunt Paige nodded firmly, as if the matter was already settled. In her mind, it probably was.

Visiting Mom is always difficult. "Difficult": that word doesn't even begin to describe it, but if I tried to write what I really felt I'd just start crying. And I promised myself, a long time ago, that I would never cry over my mom again.

Even while I waited to be admitted—standing in the familiar spacious entry hall of the medical facility, with its smell of pine, lavender, and the strongest bleach you can get—I felt a mixture of hope and despair. I can't help hoping, even after all this time, that Mom will somehow get better.

As if by magic. Yeah, wouldn't that be something to see.

So it turned out that I lost both my parents after Dad rescued me from the dark elves—after the Wood Monster ruined my hands and forever marked me as different. Mom was in the group of alchemists following behind, the ones who tried to stop Dad from getting himself killed. That's what Aunt Paige has told me; I hardly remember anything that happened that night. I was very young, and it's almost as though there's a gray cloud over the whole thing in my mind.

And then there are the dreams. But I don't even know which parts are real and which I made up.

We do know that the elves did something to Mom—worked their mojo on her while she was in their territory—but nobody knows quite what they did. Which means it can't be undone. Quentin says if the alchemists could be certain of what actually happened, they would have a better chance of fixing it. Of fixing her.

Maker's best guess was that they took a lock of her hair during the fight. An elflock is a particularly powerful kind of magic; dark fey can use a lock of human hair to invade the victim's dreams and slowly drive them mad. Seems pretty obvious to me that's what happened, but, even if that is the case, we'd need to know where that lock of hair is in order to have any chance of healing her.

So until then, she has to stay in this halfway state, here at the Institute. Most of the time she sits and stares out the window. She likes to see the sky, I think. Sometimes she's completely comatose, while other times you can at least have a conversation with her. You never know if she'll remember who you are, though.

It was good to see her today, despite everything. I was surprised at how relieved I was just to be able to sit with her. To hold her hand and look into her eyes. Her lovely eyes that are still that unusual silver-gray—my eyes do a poor imitation of them, though I remember that Dad used to compare us and say that it was our eyes that made us look like sisters. She would laugh at that.

Memories are stupid things. Why is it that I can only remember the useless stuff?

Mom's beautiful red hair has faded, and the streak of white in the front had spread since the last time I was here. I picked up the heavy brush on the old-fashioned dresser and began to run it through her long curls. I took one section at a time, working gradually and methodically until her hair shone like burnished wood.

She suffered my attentions in silence, and I wondered if she thought I was just another one of her caretakers.

But for the first time in months, it seemed as though she might actually remember who I am. As I moved to return the brush to the dresser, she clutched my hand and tried to say something— only the words wouldn't come. At least, not at first. Not until she suddenly sat forward in her chair and stared into my eyes with such intensity that it scared the crap out of me. She sat like that for ages—it seemed like hours, though of course it was only a minute or two. Neither of us spoke, and I felt my heart beat so fast. Maybe she was remembering something.

Mom said, "We tried to save you."

Over and over again, just those five words:

"We tried to save you."

And then, while she was still speaking—chanting the words like a mantra—she went to her bedside table and opened the top drawer. She rummaged inside for what seemed like ages, finally pulling out a small wooden jewelry box. She flipped it open and retrieved a tiny pouch from inside, and then pressed the soft black velvet into my hands.

"We tried to save you," she said, nodding her head firmly as though confirming it to herself. "We tried to save you."

Eventually, a nurse came and had to sedate her because she was getting so agitated. They tried to make me leave but there was no way I was going anywhere, not if there was a chance she might say something else.

What was she talking about? Save me from what? The elves? I wish she could've said more—it was the closest I've ever come to hearing something from her that seems connected to that night.

I sat by her bed, listening to the sound of her breathing and the occasional twitches and murmurs that she made even in sleep. The pouch she'd given me held a beautiful, delicately crafted silver charm bracelet. It jingled when I held it up to the light and shook it. I pushed it into my jeans pocket, safely back inside its small pouch, and resolved to examine it properly later. I know the bracelet has to be important, but right then all I wanted to do was to sit with Mom.

I watched her beautiful, ravaged face as it slowly settled into calm lines once more.

One day I will find out what happened to her, and I will figure out a way to get her back.

Seven

Donna tried not to feel nervous as she waited for Alexander Grayson in the middle of Ironbridge Common. She had dreamed her way through the day's classes
with Alma, and the tutor had even commented on her
pupil's lack of attention. Donna didn't think she could be
blamed, though. Monday's classes were usually made up
of "regular" lessons, the things that she should be covering
in high school; how was she supposed to concentrate on
the Declaration of Independence when she had a sort-of
date with a ridiculously gorgeous guy?

The precise center point of the Common was a regular meeting place for friends and lovers. Donna's eyes strayed to the old wooden bandstand as she sat down on an unoccupied bench. She felt suddenly self-conscious and scruffy in her frayed jeans, although she had added a fitted silver tunic and her favorite black velvet gloves when she changed, after class, in one of the luxurious bathrooms in Quentin Frost's huge house. Her thick gray woolen coat and flat silver pumps completed the outfit, while her hair had been simply and hastily brushed and left loose. It was growing fast, already almost to her shoulders. Seeing her mother's crazy-long tresses last night had made Donna want to get all her hair cut off again, as she'd done last year, much to her aunt's horror.

She couldn't remember the last time she'd felt this nervous; she cursed her weak stomach as it flip-flopped and somersaulted. The cold November air forced her to huddle further into her coat, and she wished she'd worn boots. All of this concern over hair and wardrobe wasn't Donna's usual style, but at least it gave her something else to worry about.

The Common was busy, even this late on a Monday afternoon; people were returning from the newly opened shopping mall and the surrounding shops, while others were no doubt out to enjoy their evenings after school. Darkness had already fallen, cloaking the treetops in indigo velvet; the only light came from the strategically positioned lampposts lining each pathway. No moon was visible tonight, and the stars were covered by a blanket of cloud.

Donna fiddled with the charm bracelet that was now clasped around her wrist. It had been in her pocket all day, tucked inside its velvet pouch. She wondered why her mother had given it to her and what it meant. When she'd examined it, in the privacy of her bedroom, she'd felt a familiar tingle as soon as the metal touched her palm. One thing she was certain of: the bracelet held magic in its silver, intricately carved charms. She desperately wanted to ask Aunt Paige if she knew of the bracelet's significance, but it was so rare for something out of the ordinary to happen when she visited her mother that she just wanted to clutch this slight memory to herself. At least for a little while longer. Her aunt would see the bracelet soon enough, if she decided to start wearing it regularly.

And then, all thought of potentially magical bracelets was swept from her mind as Xan came striding toward her with his hands shoved deep into the pockets of a long black coat, his thick amber hair catching the light as he passed the lampposts.

"Sorry I'm late." His voice was breathless, as if he'd been hurrying.

"It's cool." Donna tried to smile, but found that her mouth wasn't working properly. She sounded as breathless as he did, yet she'd been sitting here for the last ten minutes.

Xan stood in front of her. "So, do you want to sit out in the cold, or shall we go and find that coffee?"

"Let's get coffee." Maybe if she kept her responses to a minimum, she wouldn't sound like such an idiot.

They walked side by side in companionable silence for a while, Donna stealing occasional glances at Xan. He kept his head down, watching the leaf-strewn path ahead of them, which was handy when it came to guiding her out of the way of a pile of broken glass. She slid her hands into the pockets of her coat—not for warmth, but because she was afraid she might reach out to take his hand.

"So, where are we going?" she asked.

"*Coffee*. Wow, you've got a short memory, Donna Underwood."

She flashed him a mock glare. "You know what I mean."

"I thought we could try Mildred's. We might just slip in and get a seat between the day and night shifts."

"Okay, cool." Donna was amazed at how ordinary her voice sounded, as though walking through Ironbridge Common with a hot guy was the most normal thing in the world. She glanced up and caught him staring at her with an almost hungry expression. Wrenching her gaze away, she wondered if she was making a mistake, meeting this strange young man she barely knew.

But as her stomach fluttered and her cheeks burned, she thought, *How can I possibly resist?*

The pathway Xan had chosen wound past a small collection of trees; there were maybe a couple dozen newly planted ones alongside half-grown saplings. The intermittent lampposts lighting the way seemed to be spaced farther apart here, hardly making an impression on the early evening darkness.

There were fewer people in this part of the Common, and it was still pretty far from the main road. If Donna strained hard enough, she could hear muffled car engines beyond the undergrowth, but otherwise the sounds surrounding them were from nature—birds calling to one another as they finished settling in for the evening, and a mysterious, indefinable, low-pitched vibration that was sort of froglike. Really, Donna's knowledge of wildlife was pathetic, but it was refreshing to walk in the sharp air with Xan beside her, just taking in the scenery.

He seemed at peace out here, his hands still resting deep in his pockets and his head up, green eyes alert and shining.

Donna was the first to break the silence. "So, is this a regular shortcut?"

Xan glanced at her. "Yeah, it saves walking around the whole northeast corner; it's much—"

But she never did find out what he was going to say because a man-sized shape flung itself at him and knocked him off his feet. Donna heard the air forced out of Xan's lungs, a surprised sound that was cut off, almost immediately, as whoever attacked put his big hands around Xan's throat.

"Xan!" Donna ran toward the two bodies, which were rolling around and scattering dried leaves and a nest of sleeping squirrels in their wake.

Xan seemed to have gained the upper hand and was now on top of his attacker. Donna spared a moment to wonder how he'd managed that so quickly, but all thought was forgotten when she got her first real look at the...*person* Xan was fighting. At first glance, he could pass for a regular homeless dude; just another guy from the street, complete with ratty-looking coat and several scarves muffling his face. Donna caught glimpses of his lined white skin and bushy dark beard before he broke free of the chokehold and pushed himself back to his feet.

Xan flipped himself upright with super-fast agility that took Donna's breath away. What the hell? How did he do that?

But before she could get any further, Crazy Homeless Dude grabbed her arm and pulled her against him. She thought he would stink something awful, but in fact all she could smell was rich earth and the faint aroma of damp umbrellas.

"Get off me!" Donna struggled against him, but her back was mashed against the guy's chest and he had both arms around her, pinning her arms to her sides.

Xan was half-crouched in front of them, his hair sticking up and his eyes burning emerald-bright in the near darkness. "Take your hands off her, man." His voice was low and vibrated with barely repressed fury.

Donna heard the emotion underneath Xan's words as easily as she heard her own panicked breathing. It gave her courage, somehow, knowing that this guy she'd only just met wanted to protect her.

But there was something very important that Xan didn't know about her. Donna Underwood didn't need protection. Not when she had alchemical magic running through her arms and hands.

Not when she was a freak of nature.

Sucking in a steadying breath, she squeezed her hands into fists and pushed outward with both arms. The scruffy dude holding on to her was strong, but Donna bet that she was stronger. Her attacker gave a surprised cry as she dislodged him. He stumbled backward, trying to keep his balance as he stepped over a fallen branch.

Now it was Xan's turn to watch *her* with astonishment. Donna felt good that she could take care of herself. It wasn't often she felt thankful for being different, but this was one of those times.

Donna and Xan now stood side by side, facing off with the vagrant who seemed intent on taking them down. What the hell was a street guy doing attacking a pair of kids? Donna wasn't stupid enough to think it was a bizarre, chance encounter. She spared Xan a glance. "You take that side, I'll take the other. Maybe together, we can hold him."

Xan's eyebrows shot up. "I knew there was something I liked about you."

And then they were circling their would-be attacker as he lunged forward once more. All three of them met in a clash of bodies that Donna felt all the way down to her toes. She was thrown to one side, unable to keep hold of the flailing arm that threatened to take her head off. So much for her plan…

She risked a glance at the nearest pathway, realizing that in the minutes they had been fighting off Crazy Homeless Dude, not a single person had passed by—or if they had, they certainly weren't stopping. It was more likely that nobody had even seen them, tucked away in the shadows of the foliage and half-grown trees way back here.

It was the perfect place for an ambush.

Xan was on the ground again; the big man had him pinned and it didn't look like he'd get free anytime soon. Donna looked around for a branch or something else she could use as a weapon, but it was hard to see clearly in the dark and the constant movement and fighting made things all the more confusing.

Her eyes came to rest on the street guy's hands as they forced Xan's head back against the cracked earth. There was a strange sort of blurring happening around them—a soft glow of light that didn't belong—almost as though she'd just woken up and her eyes weren't working properly yet. Xan was still struggling wildly, making it hard to focus, but there was no mistaking the weird haze surrounding the attacker's hands and face—the only two visible parts of his body, given how bundled up in Goodwill clothing he was.

"Xan, get away from him!" Donna called, her voice shaking. Of course, that was exactly what Xan was trying to do, but she couldn't help herself. An awful feeling was crawling from her stomach up into her chest. Her arms were starting to ache horribly, and the sensation of pins and needles in her fingers made tears stand out in her eyes.

Crazy Homeless Dude lowered his head to Xan's face and…what the hell was he doing? Donna watched with repulsion as the man's teeth suddenly seemed sharper, like there were too many of them to fit properly in his mouth.

That's not a homeless dude, Donna thought. This wasn't just a random street guy trying to mug them.

The hands now squeezing Xan's throat began to look more like claws. As Donna focused her full attention on the two figures scuffling on the cold ground, she saw right through the wood elf's glamour.

No, this couldn't be happening. Not here—here on the Common while she was on a date. Only her "date" was being attacked by a creature with too many teeth and an otherworldly strength that was completely out of proportion to its size; its *true* size. Because now that she could see through the elfskin, Donna saw that Crazy Homeless Dude's clothes were all part of the illusion—none of it was real—and Xan had a wood elf sitting on his chest, digging its claws into his wrists and trying to reach his throat with its razor-sharp teeth.

"Stop!" she yelled, running forward, ignoring the pain stabbing at her arms. The elf was in its natural habitat—surrounded by grass and trees, with no buildings or cars or other man-made structures to trouble it. No iron.

No iron, Donna thought, *except for the iron in my own body*. Pushing down the rising terror that made her feel like she might vomit, she pulled the velvet glove from her right hand and ran toward this creature from her nightmares. This was the second one that had stepped out of those dreams in as many days, and now she knew there was something serious happening. No more wondering about chance strays or Maker's "experiments"—this was something else.

And it was very, very real.

The clouds chose *that* moment to part. The waxing moon shone down and its light flashed on the tattoos winding along the back of Donna's hand. Her flesh was barely visible through the silvery patterns that were stamped permanently into it. Xan was too busy to notice anything at the moment, but that didn't mean he wouldn't find out the truth the moment she grabbed the wood elf.

Well, there were worse things. One of them would be seeing Xan hurt by the creature, and she wasn't going to let that happen.

The elf's black eyes flickered in her direction as Donna approached, but it was too late for it to stop her and she was already on top of it. She gripped its spindly arm and gritted her teeth against the pain that settled into the bones of her fingers.

As the pure iron in her hands made contact with the fey flesh of the dark elf, smoke belched from the twiggy surface of its shoulder and the creature howled with inhuman fury. It released Xan and tried to bat Donna away with its free hand. She dodged out of reach—just in time—but kept hold of the elf and pulled it farther away from Xan. She tried not to think about the smell of burning wood. Her eyes watered as the smoke filled the air, and her alarm grew as she saw how high the curling cloud had already risen. *Crap*. Lighting bonfires on Ironbridge Common was illegal, and the last thing they needed was a park warden turning up to see what was going on.

Xan stumbled to his feet, brushing himself off and staring at Donna with amazement. Not horror, she was relieved to note, but something more like admiration. And something else, too, but she couldn't quite place what it was. She wasn't sure if it was good or bad, but his eyes flashed viridian-bright in the darkness as he watched her grapple with the screeching elf.

Before she could think about it further, the creature got its other hand around her forearm—still covered by the thick wool of her coat—and tried to free itself.

Xan was suddenly there, too, and the thing didn't stand a chance after that. They got it pressed against a narrow tree trunk between them, and Xan whipped off his long black coat and threw it over the elf's head.

Donna wondered if Xan was still seeing a homeless guy, but she doubted the elfskin had held once she'd gotten hold of the creature with the full force of her iron-clad hands. She wondered how Xan was coping with the revelation that monsters existed; was this the second time she was going to have to explain all of this craziness to a friend?

And yet...Xan hadn't exactly looked shocked.

Just as Donna thought it was over, with the elf subdued beneath Xan's coat and Xan sitting on top of it while Donna pulled her glove back on with shaking hands, the elf somehow wriggled free and leapt to its feet. Damn, those things were slippery.

The coat was now hampering Xan more than the elf—he couldn't get hold of the creature before it bolted into the nearest gap between two saplings. The coat caught on a branch, and the wood elf was off and running.

However, Xan—as well as being incredibly agile and undaunted by an inhuman opponent—was *fast*. He dashed after the fleeing wood elf, leaving Donna to wait, her heart pushing its way into her throat with each passing moment. She wondered if she should follow them, but she was pretty certain she wouldn't be able to keep up. And maybe she'd get lost, and then she might not find Xan at all. Biting her lip and rubbing her arms to keep warm, she was just beginning to doubt her decision to stay put when

Xan's bright hair appeared from a different place in the small patch of trees.

He didn't seem particularly out of breath, but his cheeks were flushed, probably more from the cold than from exertion. They looked at each other across the short distance that separated them.

What did it all mean? Donna fought down panic and tried to think of the best way to approach this—should she admit to knowing what the creature was?

Xan broke eye contact first and collected his coat from the shrubs. He dusted it off and shrugged it back on, running both hands through his hair as he looked at the ground for a long moment.

"Xan—" she said.

"Donna—"

They both stopped.

Xan walked toward her. "Ladies first."

She frowned. "What happened to…you know…"

"Oh, you mean the *elf*?" His voice was filled with loathing, but she was pretty certain it wasn't directed at her. She somehow knew that the clear note of disgust was aimed solely at the elves.

Okay, so he knew what the creature was. *Alexander Grayson knew what a freaking wood elf was.* And this evening was now officially weirder than ever. Not knowing what to say, Donna kept her mouth shut and just watched him. She hardly knew Xan, but something connected them. She had a horrible feeling that she was going to find out what it was, sooner rather than later.

Xan suddenly stumbled, pain flashing across his face as he clutched his ribs. Her heart pounding, Donna ran to his side and hovered there, unsure whether or not she should touch him.

"What happened?" she asked, feeling useless as he winced and bent over, breathing hard.

He held out a hand. "Don't," he said, strain making his voice weak. "It's nothing."

"Nothing?" She was suddenly angry. At the party he had seemed so keen to get close to her, and now he was holding her at arm's length. Literally. "You're hurt, let me see—"

Xan knocked her hand away. "I said, it's nothing. That thing bit me before it escaped. I almost had it."

At least he could stand straight again, and Donna realized that the anger she'd heard in his voice was born not just of pain, but of frustration—disappointment that the creature had gotten away.

"It *bit* you?" She tried to pull open his coat to see. "Where? Oh Xan, those things are vicious…"

"Yeah," he replied, stepping out of her reach. "And you seem to know a *lot* about them."

Donna chewed on her lip. She was worried about Xan—about how badly hurt he might be—but she was also terrified about revealing too much of herself. It seemed like someone had declared open season on her most carefully guarded secrets, and she didn't like it.

She didn't like it one bit.

"Listen." She raised her chin and looked Xan fiercely in the eye. "Yes, I know things about them—but so do you. And *you're* the one who said we had stuff to talk about. That's why we're out here in the first place."

"So let's talk." It sounded like a challenge.

"I'm not talking about this stuff out here—no way."

"There's nobody to hear us, Donna." Xan gestured around them at the empty trees and the deserted pathway.

Donna swallowed, feeling suddenly very alone. She wished that Navin was here, which was pretty dumb considering how hard she'd tried to protect him from all the craziness. "I'm cold and I'm scared, Xan. I don't want to talk here."

He winced again, touching his ribs as though gingerly testing them. "Sorry, you're right. I'm being a jerk. Let's go to my place."

She only hesitated for a moment. "As long as you let me see where it hurt you."

A lopsided smile replaced the pained expression on his face. "You just want to see me with my shirt off."

Donna felt her cheeks flush. "You wish. Come on, let's get moving."

She turned away from him and headed back to the path, trying to pretend she couldn't hear the soft laughter behind her.

Eight

As they turned onto the wide residential street lined with oak trees and townhouses, the hair on the back of Donna's neck prickled. She glanced behind them, but saw nothing out of the ordinary. She tried to shake the feeling that someone was following them, but found herself turning around every so often, trying to catch a glimpse of a pursuing shadow.

It was no wonder she'd gotten so paranoid—now she had *proof* that there were wood elves sneaking around the city (not that the one on the Common had been doing much sneaking). It had been such a long time since the dark fey last entered Ironbridge; they must have their reasons, but Donna wasn't certain she wanted to know about them.

She shivered in the evening air.

"We're here," Xan said, stopping halfway up the street.

They stood in front of the familiar three-story house, almost identical to its neighbors except for the bright window shutters. Donna couldn't tell what color they were in the shadow-strewn lamplight, but they looked like they might be crimson. The place seemed different, somehow, from the way it had looked on Saturday night. She couldn't quite put her finger on it, but it was something to do with the fact that back then, she'd been with Navin and, no matter how much she'd protested going to the stupid party in the first place, there had been an element of adventure about the whole event.

But this time? This time things were very different, and this was certainly no adventure.

Xan walked up the three stone steps and took a bunch of keys out of his jeans pocket. "Well, come on then."

Donna took a deep breath, realizing that she'd been staring at the windows. She was still on the sidewalk, and Xan was holding open the front door.

"Sorry," she said. "I was just trying to figure out how to get the lid back on." The image of Pandora's Box had come to mind—there was no getting away from it now, and not just with Navin. It seemed she was being forced to let people into her life, no matter what the Order of the Dragon wanted.

His face twisted with confusion. "Um…what lid?"

She smiled and shook her head. "Nothing, forget it."

Xan was still frowning at her as she walked past him and into the house.

"There." Donna put the finishing touches on the medical dressing. "All finished."

Xan raised an eyebrow. "Not bad. First time?"

Dammit, she thought. Another guy in her life who could do that eyebrow thing. She willed herself not to blush and, for once, managed to stay composed. Xan really was very good looking, with cheekbones a model would kill for. Just sitting this close to him—on his *bed*—made her skin vibrate.

They were in Xan's bedroom again; he'd said the medical supplies were in the upstairs bathroom, and Donna had chosen to believe him. She didn't think he was just trying to lure her back to his room, not when he was bleeding all over the place. She'd refused to talk about elves and insisted on seeing his injury before anything else. Not that she was a first aid expert, but she at least knew *something* about the sort of damage the creatures could inflict.

Donna had tried really hard not to think about how toned Xan's chest was while examining the imprint of the elf's jagged teeth. This wasn't the time to act like a teenager. *But I am a teenager*, she'd wanted to shout. It was so unfair— why did these things have to happen? Why couldn't she just have a normal life? And then she immediately felt angry with herself for the blast of self-pity. She was determined to accept whatever life had to throw at her.

Of course, despite her good intentions, she didn't always succeed.

Xan had lifted up his gray button-down shirt so she could get to the cuts along the ribs on his left side. There was already a livid bruise against his golden skin, but the flesh had only been broken in a couple places.

As she packed the bandages away, Donna's mind immediately turned to what came next. Did they have to have the Big Talk? Something had brought this beautiful guy into her life, and she was both terrified and excited to find out why.

"Donna, look at me." There was that thread of vulnerability in Xan's voice again. "I have to show you something. It…might be easier than just talking. You want to understand how I know about those things, right? Know about the fey?"

When she didn't reply, he stepped in front of the bedroom door and began unbuttoning his shirt.

"What are you doing?" Donna heard how thin and breathless her voice sounded. "We already dealt with the wound."

"Oh, come *on*." He let out a frustrated breath. "What the hell do you take me for?"

She laughed, nervously. "Sorry."

"Just let me do this." Xan continued to work on the buttons, his eyes fixed on hers. It was intense and weird, and she wondered if she should feel more afraid.

"Wait a minute," she said finally. "I think we're having a misunderstanding here ..."

"Shut up, will you? Trust me." His tone made her stop. What was it about this guy that made her *want* to trust him?

Xan's fingers looked steady as he got to the top button of the shirt. He turned to face the door, so that his back was toward her, and allowed the shirt to slide off his shoulders and fall softly to the floor.

The skin on his back was as smooth and golden as it was on his chest. He was broad-shouldered, and his muscles were lean and sculpted. His waist tapered neatly to the top of his jeans.

But it was none of this that held Donna's attention. None of this that made her gasp with shock and a strange sort of recognition.

Above Xan's shoulder blades lay two livid scars, several inches long, covered with bumpy scar tissue. White, pink, and magenta. The palette of colors told the old and painful story of a gradual healing process. The scars stood out starkly against the warm tone of his skin.

With one hand to her mouth, Donna stepped forward despite her horror. She had to *see*. If he was going to trust her—someone he hardly even *knew*—with this, she could at least show the respect such a revelation deserved. She stood within touching distance, wanting desperately to reach out to Xan in that moment. Her hand wavered, then settled back against her fluttering belly.

Up close, she could see twisted ropes of scar tissue deep beneath his flesh, not just across the surface. Whatever it was that had happened must have hurt like hell. It was unimaginable. Well, maybe not unimaginable... She felt a sympathetic twinge in her hands and arms as she craned her neck in the dim light to examine the badly healed wounds. Sadness tightened her throat at the thought that his healing had come with such terrible scars. It made her feel a rush of gratitude toward Maker, for the care she'd received after her own terrible injuries.

Releasing a painful breath, Donna brought her attention back to the room. Back to Xan.

"What happened?" Her voice was low but steady.

"I think you already know." Xan's voice was muffled, his back a painful map of loss and history.

Shaking her head, even though she knew he couldn't see her, Donna tried to reply. "No, I don't know. I *don't*."

"It's where they tore out my wings."

"Wings," she echoed, faintly.

Xan turned to face her, turning those dreadful scars away so she no longer had to look at them. He bent down to pick up the discarded shirt and hastily shrugged his way back into it, leaving it unbuttoned.

She stood there for a moment, motionless, allowing herself to breathe slowly and evenly. Be calm, she told herself. You can be calm in the face of this.

Another thought came to her: *Isn't it interesting that I don't doubt him? Not for a second.* She could thank her twisted upbringing for that.

"You're not saying much," Xan said, all traces of his earlier confidence wiped from his face. There was a deep frown-line between his brows, and his eyes looked heavy and tired. Shadows danced on the planes of his cheeks and the dip of his throat.

"I don't know what to say." Donna gestured with one gloved hand, trying to find the right words. "I don't understand why you're showing me this. Xan, your *back*—"

Xan shrugged. "I'm used to it now."

Donna felt a pain in her chest, one that almost matched the ache in the bones of her hands and arms. "No you're not," she said. "How can you ever be? Nobody could get used to that."

"How can *you* know that?"

"Because I'm speaking from experience."

And Donna did the thing she'd never imagined that she would do. She swallowed, then carefully and slowly peeled off her long velvet gloves, feeling not unlike a burlesque act. Except an experienced burlesque dancer's hands wouldn't be shaking as much as hers were right now. She tossed her hair back and tried to meet Xan's eyes as she held both hands out, palms down, in front of her.

It was one of the hardest things she had ever done.

From mid-forearm to the tips of her fingers, Donna's arms and hands were covered with swirling silver artwork. It was as if a tattoo artist had created a spectacular silver pigment and used it to ink her arms in intricate whorls and curves; curls that extended down to her wrists, and then across the backs of her hands and down each finger. If you looked quickly, there was the illusion that her hands and arms were made of metal—it was only when you looked properly that you realized a delicate pattern enclosed her flesh.

What people wouldn't know was that the marks were the result of magical wardings branded not just onto the surface of Donna's skin, but *inside* as well. There had been operations when she was a child, magical operations that she chose not to think about. Not because there had been pain at the time, but because of the strange cold metal that now encased her bones. Maker might be a master craftsman, but Donna sometimes had a hard time appreciating his work when it made her feel so *cold*.

But this strange beauty was part of her now, forever. Her skin never itched or tanned under the sun, or scalded if the water was too hot.

Xan didn't say a word for what felt like a lifetime. Donna swallowed hard and forced herself to look at him as he drank in the sight of her. He was transfixed by the shimmering silver spirals that wound around her wrists and up toward her elbows.

His eyes shone brighter than ever as he looked at her. "I knew there must be a reason that I met you. You're like me. You *understand*."

Donna couldn't help a small, sad smile. "And you understand me, too." She pulled on her gloves again, concentrating on the task so as not to see the warmth in Xan's gaze. There was a buzzing sound in her ears and she felt lightheaded.

"Thank you," Xan said, his voice grave.

"For what?"

"For trusting me."

Donna shrugged awkwardly as silence fell between them again, making her wonder if she had just made a terrible mistake. What was she doing? Had she lost her mind? As she contemplated the state of her sanity, the silence stretched and took on a new quality. It felt loaded with something heavier—somehow more real—and Donna wasn't sure she wanted to let the moment unfold. She shifted uncomfortably.

"I still don't know what to say to you, Xan." She nibbled at her lower lip. "I mean...my life has had some pretty strange things in it, but up until now a guy with wings wasn't one of them."

"I don't have wings anymore," he said, his voice hollow.

"Sorry, I just…" She shook her head, unable to continue. What could she say? She forced a smile. "Don't tell me you're some kind of fallen angel, please. Because, you know, I don't think I could handle that."

Xan barked out a short laugh. "You mean you could handle something else?"

"I don't think I believe in angels, that's all. And if you were one, that would mean I'd have to re-evaluate my beliefs. I'm not quite ready to do that."

"You're in the clear, Donna Underwood. I'm certainly no angel." A smile spread slowly across his face.

She laughed, a strained release of tension more than anything else. "Phew."

They stood in silence for a moment longer.

But Donna couldn't help herself. She had to say it. "So, you're fey, then." Because really, what else *could* he be?

He started, surprise in his eyes, then something that looked a lot like relief. He drew in a shaky breath. "Only half."

"Half fey." She nodded, confirming something to herself. Of course, she knew that there were half-fey beings walking among humans. Apart from the interspecies mating that must have happened over the course of centuries, even before the faeries had left this world for good, there were the small numbers of solitary fey left behind. So it wasn't inconceivable that there would be some half-faery kids wandering around, hidden among their human cousins. But she had never imagined that any of those children would have *actual wings*.

Or *should* have had wings. Her throat constricted with sorrow; sadness for what Xan had lost, but also for how alone he must feel. Her eyes flickered to the clock by his bed—the same one she'd seen when she was first here, Saturday night. It seemed like so long ago, and yet only two days had passed.

Donna felt so tired. Her shoulders ached and her throat was scratchy. She hoped she wasn't coming down with something. "I have to go. I'm having a late dinner at Navin's tonight—his father invited me. I was only supposed to meet you for a coffee."

Xan was too polite to point out how obvious it was that she'd made late plans with her friend as a safety net, an escape route from coffee with a stranger.

"Always dashing off, just like Cinderella." His face showed disappointment, but he helped her on with her coat and straightened her collar. "I still don't know anything about you."

"I just showed you something that would beg to differ."

Xan pushed his hair out of his eyes. His bangs looked as though they needed cutting. "Seeing is one thing, but I'm left making guesses and not coming up with a lot that makes sense."

She sighed. "I know. I'm sorry."

"So," he said. "Can you meet me tomorrow?"

He was insistent, she had to give him that. "I guess…"

"Thanks for sounding so enthusiastic." A smile touched his lips.

Donna wondered how on earth Xan could find anything to smile about at a time like this. "I didn't mean it that way. I'm just finding this—"

He raised his eyebrows. "Hot?"

"I was going to say intense," she replied, tempted to hit him.

"*And* hot?" His voice held a wistful note, but she knew he was just teasing her. Why did guys have to do that, anyway? She shook her head and decided to ignore it. "I'll meet you after my classes tomorrow."

Xan insisted on walking her back across the Common. She didn't protest this, not after their run-in with the elf. There were no further incidents, although she'd caught her breath when they passed a young homeless guy sleeping on a bench under a newsprint blanket.

It was getting late and she was drained, half-wishing she didn't have dinner plans. If they had just been with Navin, he'd understand her need for a quiet night, but they were with Navin's family, and she didn't want to let his father down on such short notice. It had been kind of him to invite her and, anyway, she really *did* want to check whether Navin was okay. She had to see for herself that he wasn't slowly going nuts with all his new knowledge. All the craziness.

Truth be told, Donna really just needed to know that Navin was still her friend.

The moon-sliver hung high in the obsidian sky. She kept glancing at her companion striding along so quietly beside her. *I'm falling for him*, Donna thought fiercely. And then: *That's ridiculous*. She probably only felt so drawn to him because of the things they had in common. That made far more sense.

Giving herself a mental shake as they passed through the gates at the edge of the Common, she turned to Xan. "You can leave me here, now. Thanks. It's not much farther."

"Let me walk you all the way home." They stood, looking at one another.

"You'd better not."

"Ah." He looked serious. "You don't want your *friend* to see us together." His intimation was clear.

"Navin *is* my friend, I told you." She tried to push down the annoyance she felt tightening her chest. "It's just…I haven't told him about you, yet."

Xan's brows drew together. "He met me on Saturday."

"I mean, he doesn't know I was seeing you tonight."

"So you're going to tell him." It sounded like a challenge.

"Maybe. What I do or don't tell Nav is none of your business."

She saw a muscle working in his jaw. He looked about to say something, but then stopped, took a visibly deep breath, and rubbed a hand over his face. "Right. Of course. I just wish we could spend more time together, that's all."

She nodded and decided to let it go. He was pretty intense and that could be scary, but under the circumstances it was hard to blame him. "It's okay. Good night. I'll see you tomorrow."

"Good night—" He took a step toward her.

Donna backed away, almost tripping over the edge of the pathway where it joined the sidewalk. Turning quickly, she walked home without looking back.

Nine

"That was the best meal I've had in *ages*," Donna said, her stomach full to bursting. Despite how tired she felt, she was happy, after all, that this dinner had been scheduled. "Thank you for going to so much trouble, Dr. Sharma."

"No trouble at all, Donna. Always a pleasure to have you sit at our table." Navin's father smiled benevolently at Donna and his two children, frowning when his usually mild gaze came to rest on his daughter.

Nisha, her head down, was busy texting. Her long black hair shone under the lights, looking to Donna like a raven's wing. Donna gave her a gentle prod under the table.

Nisha's big brown eyes flashed with annoyance, but when she noticed that her father was giving her a stern look, her expression softened. Glancing gratefully at Donna, she slipped the cell phone into the pocket of her skinny jeans, having to half-stand to do so, but at least Dr. Sharma looked mollified.

Hiding a smirk, Navin started to clear the table and Donna quickly rose to join him. Dr. Sharma stopped them with a sweep of his arm. "Don't worry about that today, son—you attend to your guest. Nisha and I will do the dishes."

Nisha shot Navin a glare, but didn't argue.

Donna tried not to smile at being referred to as Navin's "guest." She'd been coming over to visit for three years, yet Dr. Sharma still treated her like an honored guest each time she was here. It was sort of nice, she had to admit.

Upstairs in Navin's tiny bedroom, she lay down on the bed to stretch her stomach. "That was an amazing curry." It felt good to be doing something normal with her friend. She even dared let herself believe that everything would be okay between them.

"Yeah," Navin agreed, sorting through an untidy stack of CDs. "He and Mom often cooked together when we were younger. Now he says he's glad he didn't leave it all to her or he'd be pretty useless now."

Donna smiled. "He does a great job."

Navin came and sat at the end of the bed, leaning against the wall. They listened to the quiet music—a movie soundtrack Navin was currently very excited about—and Donna allowed the comfort of just being together to ease her worried mind.

"Nav…" She sat up and leaned against the headboard.

Navin's brown eyes were soft as he waited for her to speak. He was giving her time, which she sort of appreciated, but on the other hand, she wished he would make everything easier and fill the gap for her.

Sighing, she reached out and took his hand in hers. "I'm so glad you let me come over tonight."

He frowned. "Dad wanted you to come—why would I get in the way of that?"

"Oh Nav, you know why. After everything I told you…" Her voice trailed off and she stared at the psychedelic screensaver flashing across his computer monitor. Anything to avoid his gaze. How could she tell him that she didn't think she could go on if he wasn't her best friend any more?

Navin touched her chin and gently drew her around to face him. "It's all right, Donna. I'm not saying this is easy—getting my head around everything and readjusting my whole worldview—but I'm doing my best. And I'm still here, okay?"

Donna felt a warm glow spread through her chest, pushing away the last cold threads of fear. "You're so important to me. You know that, right?"

He smiled. "Wow, you must be stressed, Underwood. Admitting your true feelings for me? I should get that recorded."

Donna gave him a shove, being careful to hold back. "That was pathetic. Call yourself a superhero?"

"Oh, ha ha. You're so funny. Maybe you could be my sidekick, Sink Plunger Boy."

"Nah, girls make far better sidekicks than guys," jibed Navin, giving her a hard push back. "You should learn your place, you know?"

A full-scale fight ensued—more tickling than anything else, but totally fun and probably way too noisy. In the midst of it, Donna wondered briefly if they might be too old for this, and she was also conscious of Dr. Sharma and Nisha not all that far away. But then she decided, *What the hell.*

Gasping for breath, Donna finally pulled away and sat up to smooth her wayward hair and straighten her sweater. "You're such a pushover, Sharma."

"Oh yeah, whatever. I was holding back."

"And you think I wasn't?" She grinned evilly.

Navin sat up too, resting his elbows on his knees and watching her with a suddenly serious expression. "So, what are you going to do?"

"About what?" Her mind had wandered back to Xan—to the smooth skin of his stomach, a cruel contrast to those terrible scars on his back—and she shook herself guiltily.

"*All* of it." He rolled his eyes.

Donna shrugged. "I don't know. Sneaking around behind my aunt's back like this? I could be in big trouble if I don't tell her about the things I've seen the past couple days. The Order doesn't play games; you don't know what it's like."

He frowned. "Yeah, well, I *would* know if you'd start talking to me more."

She sighed. "You know it's only because I can't. And I was scared to tell you."

"*Scared*? Of what?"

"Of losing you," she said in a small voice. For a moment she wished the bed would swallow her up, as she waited for the reassurance that she'd half-convinced herself would never come.

"Hey, you're never going to lose me, Underwood—you're stuck with me for life. Do you hear me?"

Donna shrugged and tried to believe him. She hated herself for sounding so pathetic. "I was protecting you, as well. It's dangerous out there, Nav. There are things you wouldn't believe."

"I think I'd believe anything you told me, at this point. I saw an *elf* yesterday, remember?" He flashed one of those quick grins at her.

"That's true." She smiled weakly. *Was it only yesterday?*

"If it's any help, I think I'm beginning to understand why you kept so much from me."

She shifted uncomfortably on the bed. "I didn't want to hide things. I wanted to tell you *so* many times."

He shrugged. "Don't sweat it. I've been looking into things for myself now, anyway."

"You have?" Donna's temples started to hurt. Oh God, she thought, please don't let him be doing anything stupid.

"I asked my dad about alchemy, for a start."

Navin looked so proud of himself, Donna didn't know if she had the heart to burst his bubble. She thought about it for moment... yeah, maybe she did.

"Your *dad*?" she asked. "What are you asking *him* for? You do know we're well into the twenty-first century; most people who want to 'look into things' give Google a shot."

"You're a barrel of laughs tonight, you know that? Seriously, though, I knew Dad would be up on this stuff; he's totally into Indian philosophy. Apparently alchemy's been studied in India for centuries. It's really quite interesting—"

"I'm sure it is." Donna gave him a hard stare. "But maybe we could save the lessons for another time? I get enough of this at home."

"Okay, but I'm saving this stuff up for you. It's pretty cool."

Donna couldn't help smiling, but at the same time it sort of freaked her out that Navin had talked about this with his father. Sure, Dr. Sharma was cool as far as parents went, but she couldn't afford for Navin to take any risks. Not just for her sake or to protect the secrecy of the Order, but for his own safety.

"Navin, you *were* careful with what you asked, right?" Donna bit her lip, hoping she didn't sound as if she didn't trust him.

He rolled his eyes. "No, I totally blabbed all about you and the Order of the Dragon. I haven't gotten around to the dark elves yet, but give me time."

Donna blushed but let out a sigh of relief. "Shut up."

"Look, I wouldn't even have to do my own detective work if you'd open up a bit more. Surely there are things you can share now, right? You've told me as much as you have already, so there's no reason to hold back any more."

She took a deep breath. "Uh-oh, I don't like the sound of this."

He smiled nervously, pulling his knees up to his chest and wrapping his arms around them. "There's no easy way to ask this, and I'm going to sound like I've completely lost it but... I have to know." He took a visibly deep breath.

"You *are* human, aren't you, Don? Not that it matters to me, I swear. You know I'm an equal opportunities kinda guy."

Gripping her hands tightly together as she tried to ignore the hot thread of guilt running through her, Donna forced a smile. "Of course I'm human, idiot. What did you think? That I was suddenly going to grow fangs or turn into a werewolf at the next full moon?"

He shrugged, his brown cheeks gaining a cute reddish tint. "Honestly, with everything I've seen and heard? I just needed to check. Cut me some slack here."

Donna pushed down any lingering guilt—it wasn't like she was really lying to him. She *was* human. Okay, so maybe she'd been *enhanced* after her injuries, but that didn't make her less than human. At least, that's what Aunt Paige had always told her. In her aunt's view, the modifications that Maker had created to save her arms and hands made her "more than human." Which sounded a little better.

Didn't it?

"You look cute when you blush, Sharma." Teasing him seemed the best way to go.

He narrowed his eyes. "I don't blush."

"Sure you do. You're doing it right now." Donna grinned and felt some of her worries drift away as Navin's slow smile appeared, just like old times.

"You're crazy. All the magic must've gotten to you."

"I am *not* crazy."

"You must be, if you've got the hots for a college drop-out with nothing better to do than throw lame parties for kids like us."

Now it was Donna's turn, and she squirmed as her cheeks flushed. She hadn't even gotten round to mentioning Xan yet. "Shut it, Biker Boy."

So the teasing and fighting began again, and this time they *did* make too much noise and had to stop suddenly after a polite knock on the door from Dr. Sharma.

They lowered their voices and talked long into the night. Donna told Navin about the Wood Monster and the hunting elves, about the night she lost her father in the woods, about the multiple operations and magical tattoos needed to fix her injuries. It was almost as though the earlier revelations with Xan had prepared her for this, like they had been a dress rehearsal for the Big Performance. For so many years, the idea of telling Navin the awful truth had been both a dream and a nightmare for Donna; it seemed too much to hope for that he might actually still accept her.

She watched her best friend's kind and familiar face relax as she opened up to him, and prayed that she wasn't going to end up hurting him.

Back in her own room, way past curfew, Donna stripped off her clothes and threw them onto the wicker chair in the corner of her room. She pulled on pajamas and rubbed her aching arms and wrists. It felt good to get the gloves off, even if it meant she had to look at the intricate patterns. Well, it wasn't like she hadn't taken the stupid things off enough times tonight already. Maybe she should start leaving her gloves at home. See what Aunt Paige made of that.

She swallowed as she remembered the look on Navin's face when she'd finally shown him the truth—the tattoos that made her "more than human" and a lot more dangerous than your regular seventeen-year-old girl. Navin's reaction? Incredibly, he had held her hands in his and told her it didn't matter to him if she was covered from head to toe in purple paisley. She was still Donna; she was still his best friend.

He was amazing and she wondered, not for the first time, what she'd done to deserve such a good and loyal friend. Sighing, she turned on the bedside lamp and switched off the main light, going over to the window to check that it was closed against the cold. As she lifted the curtain aside, she thought she heard something outside the window; a sort of scrabbling and snuffling sound. *Now what?*

Holding her breath, Donna angled her body to cover the reflection of her lamp in the glass, the better to see outside. Her bedroom was at the back of the house, so her view consisted of a row of yards and an alleyway, with the taller buildings of downtown Ironbridge beyond that. She strained her eyes, trying to see into her aunt's pristine back yard.

Something bounded over the fence, a darting shadow with a long tail and huge eyes that caught the light of the moon. Just another damn cat. She let out a sigh of relief and determinedly pulled the curtains tightly shut. There's nothing out there, Underwood, she told herself. Just go to bed.

But of course, she couldn't sleep, and her mind kept whirring with all the things that had happened. First, there was the wood elf at Maker's. The old alchemist claimed to have "dealt with it." How he'd done that Donna wasn't sure she wanted to know, but whatever had gone down while she was there, he certainly didn't want her to tell Aunt Paige about it.

And it was odd that Maker had mentioned Simon Gaunt. Was the Order's secretary involved in whatever Maker's so-called experiments were? More importantly, could she find out for sure without alerting anyone to her suspicions?

Then there'd been the second elf that attacked her and Xan on Ironbridge Common. It was too much to hope for that it had been simple chance. Maybe it really was only a stray, but then why wasn't it in the remains of Ironwood Forest with the other strays? The fact that the targets of the attack had been a daughter of the alchemists and a human-faery hybrid indicated something a lot more sinister than simply a random encounter. Donna wasn't naïve enough to believe that two dark elves in as many days was nothing to worry about; not to mention her near-certainty that something had been watching her and Navin outside Xan's house after the party.

So why didn't she just ignore Maker's warning and spill everything to Aunt Paige? That was the big question—maybe even bigger than anything else that was happening. What was stopping her from relieving herself of this burden and handing it over to the alchemists?

Even before the tangle of questions had finished filling her overwrought mind, she knew the answer. It wasn't that she didn't trust her aunt; it was more about her growing suspicion that she couldn't trust the Order. Donna had never really been comfortable with the organization that practically ran her life—a secret society that kept secrets from her even about her own *parents*.

She had a horrible suspicion that all of these things were linked, but she didn't know how the pieces fit together. Of course, that didn't mean that she couldn't find out. Starting tomorrow.

Ten

Donna sat in Simon Gaunt's wood-panelled study at the Frost Estate, trying not to fall asleep as Alma Kensington droned on about alchemical theory. Her tutor was talking about the *prima materia*—the first matter—something that Donna knew she should be more interested in, but it was difficult to focus on anything after what had happened to her and Xan last night.

And after what she'd shared with both him *and* Navin. She hoped that her guilty conscience didn't show on her face.

Her eyes wandered to one of the many portraits of long-dead alchemists that hung around the study. It portrayed a spooky-looking dude in a black skullcap and Elizabethan robes; he had deep-set eyes and a crazy white beard. The inscription beneath read:

> WHO DOES NOT UNDERSTAND
> SHOULD EITHER LEARN
> OR BE SILENT.

These words were attributed to Dr. John Dee, mathematician, astrologer, and Master Magus. Quentin had once told her that Dee might even have been a spy for Elizabeth I in England, although those were just legends.

Donna sighed. If Dr. Dee's words should be taken to heart, she really ought to keep her mouth shut about all the things that had been happening lately—she sure as hell didn't understand them. There was a lot about the Order of the Dragon that she didn't understand, and those parts that were becoming clearer weren't exactly filling her with a warm fuzzy feeling.

Alma Kensington chose that moment to turn her ash-blonde head and fix Donna with her watery blue eyes. Her straight nose and pointed chin matched the long lines and angles of her body. "Donna, are you unwell this morning?"

Donna felt a frozen smile, more like a grimace, spread across her lips. "I'm just tired, Alma. Sorry."

Her tutor pulled herself up to her not insignificant height. "Perhaps I should speak to your aunt. This seems to be happening more often lately…" She let her voice trail off suggestively, the warning clear.

Gritting her teeth against the desire to yawn, Donna sat up straighter in the green leather chair and shook her head. She swallowed the yawn so that she could speak. "Really, I'm fine. I was up too late reading."

"Something interesting, I hope," Alma replied coolly, before turning back to the PowerPoint display on the pull-down screen.

Lunchtime couldn't come fast enough, and Donna gladly escaped her makeshift schoolroom to get some fresh air out on the vast grounds of the Frost Estate. Shivering in the cold, she wrapped her arms around herself and set off on a circuit of the gardens, taking in the gradual desolation that the approaching winter had wreaked on the beautiful plants and flowers.

The elaborately arranged flowerbeds had an underlying order and purpose that a casual observer wouldn't see: everything was laid out according to the rules of sacred geometry. It was one of Quentin's pet projects, and Aunt Paige had once told Donna that the gardens actually protected the estate from attack. There were elaborate swirls and arcs crisscrossed with diagonal lines in clashing colors. Some of the most seemingly chaotic flower arrangements were, in fact, carefully designed to mirror geometric shapes and precise angles. If viewed from the sky, the whole thing would look amazing—kind of like a secret message that only the stars could read.

In the eastern corner of the grounds, far in the distance, there was a constant curl of smoke winding its way from the ground and up into the sky. Donna had seen it there during cold weather and hot, throughout all seasons, and regardless of whether there were leaves to be burned or not. Aunt Paige had once told her it was just a bonfire, but if that was true, then why would it be burning all year round?

She returned to the house early, forcing herself to nibble on a sandwich that the kitchen staff had sent for her. She wasn't even remotely hungry, but forced herself to take a few bites as she wandered the hallways. Her mind kept flashing back to images of the wood elf attacking Xan, just as the one in Maker's workshop had attacked Navin the previous day. Blowing out a breath, she gave herself a shake and changed direction, stepping out of the way of two members of Quentin's staff who were discussing some kind of building work as they walked down one of the many richly carpeted hallways. Alma wouldn't be back yet, so Donna decided to head down to the main library for a while.

She often wondered what it would be like to live in such a grand house, which apparently had been a consideration when she was first orphaned. She usually came to the conclusion that it would be a lot more trouble than it was worth; the restrictions and sense of forced decorum here would drive her slowly insane.

And besides, living with Quentin and Simon would be *weird*.

She was always so grateful to Aunt Paige for taking in such a badly injured and traumatized child. Aunt Paige hadn't ever shown her anything but care and kindness— her own particular brand of *practical* kindness, to be sure, but that was mostly enough. If she sometimes came across as a little strict, Donna realized this was probably because her aunt had never had a husband or children of her own; she was not the most natural mother-figure. And, of course, Aunt Paige always seemed too busy for a family, what with full-time work and the demands of the Order.

Stopping at the end of a quiet corridor on the ground floor, Donna pushed through elegant doors and into Quentin Frost's favorite library. When she was younger, the archmaster had seemed like a distant, mysterious figure. *Almost magical*, which wasn't so very far from the truth.

Not that she actually saw much of Quentin, even now. He had grown more and more reclusive over the years, and Donna had only seen him perhaps half a dozen times in the past year, either at the Sunday dinners Aunt Paige encouraged her to attend or very rarely when he "came out of retirement" to teach one of her practical classes. But back when she was young, he had occasionally found her in his library browsing through the hundreds of books that lined the shelves, and he'd seemed genuinely delighted that she showed such a keen interest.

The other name for this library was the "Blue Room," for obvious reasons. The three-piece suite in the center of the large space was upholstered in the softest royal blue velvet, and the walls were a sort of duck-egg shade interspersed with tiny cornflower motifs. Personally, Donna thought the whole thing was kind of overdone, but Quentin liked to have color-themed sitting rooms.

The lounge area of the library was no exception. The couch was positioned in front of a low coffee table made of rosewood, and on *that* rested one of Quentin and Simon's favorite evening pastimes: a chess set. But it was no ordinary chess set; there was nothing regular about it beyond the beautiful checkered board. This was elemental chess, something the alchemists had developed from the traditional game. Donna still hadn't learned how to play—the pieces had different names and were associated with the stars and planets. It had always looked confusing to her, and not really like something she could imagine herself playing.

Navin would probably love it.

In one corner of the room stood a lofty grandfather clock, jammed in between two huge bookcases. She wandered over to its familiar bulk, taking in the sharp smell of wood polish and blinking her eyes against the fumes. The clock had recently been cleaned, and it gleamed under the bright ceiling spotlights.

Donna looked more closely when she realized that the clock had stopped. She checked the time on her cell phone and looked back at the ornate clock's face—yes, it appeared to have run out of juice (or whatever it ran on) about twenty minutes ago. She ran her hands along the smooth wooden casing, picking up the sticky residue of the polish on her green velvet gloves. She wondered how the clock opened, since there didn't appear to be any obvious mechanism or catch. Gazing back up at the ivory face, with its large roman numerals and its elaborately curved hands sitting still and silent, Donna placed one hand on the glass covering the timepiece and felt around for some way of opening the front. She could at least see how easy it would be to change the time.

Biting her lip in concentration, Donna stretched higher on tiptoes, both hands on the clock face as she peered around the back of the case. Perhaps somewhere *behind* the clock...

"What do you think you're doing?" said a sharp voice behind her.

If it was possible to jump any higher, Donna thought at that moment she would have done it. As it was, she leapt into the air with a shriek, then turned to face the owner of that stern voice.

"I asked you a question, young lady." Simon Gaunt's pale face pulled into grim lines, and his flint-gray eyes were narrowed with suspicion.

"Er...I..."

"*Well?*"

Donna swallowed, trying desperately to wipe the guilty look off her face and resenting how like a child he made her feel. It wasn't like she'd done anything wrong. Plus, it felt strange that the normally unflustered Simon was undeniably...flustered? Anxious, even. *Now isn't that interesting...*

She fixed her face into a mask of on-her-best-behavior. "I came here to look at the books, Simon. The Blue Room always makes me feel...um, peaceful."

"So peaceful, it seems," he replied dryly, "that you find yourself examining the furniture instead of the bookshelves."

"I was only *looking* at it, I wasn't doing any harm. I wondered how it worked, that's all." She cringed inwardly as disbelief crossed Simon's usually smooth face. "It's stopped, you see?"

He raised his perfectly groomed silver eyebrows. "Really? I had no idea you had such a burgeoning interest in horology. I must tell Quentin; I'm sure he'll be quite fascinated. You'll have something to talk about with him."

Horology? God, that sounded so boring. Donna tried to smile, walking away from the grandfather clock and nearer to the couch where she had carelessly thrown her backpack. "Hardly." She hoped she sounded more confident than she felt. "I was just curious."

"Hmm."

Simon's noncommittal grunt sounded harsh, but at least he had stopped staring at her with such outright hostility. Donna was shocked by his manner and tone. Sure, the Order's secretary was unpleasant at the best of times, but even for him this was pretty bizarre. He wasn't just angry; he seemed...scared. This crazy defensive attitude about something as innocent as a stupid clock got her thoughts humming. What was Simon trying to hide?

Any minute now, would wood elves come pouring out of the clock, breaking free from captivity after Simon and Maker's mysterious "experiments"?

Pushing aside these fantasies, Donna tried to look polite and apologetic; it would do her no good to antagonize him. "I'm sorry, Simon. I really was just interested. I'll get back to my books."

Simon looked at her backpack. "Which seem to still be in your bag, I see."

She walked to the couch on shaking legs and sat down. "Yes, here they are. I had some to return to the library."

He just stood in the doorway, watching her.

Donna tried to hold his gaze, but it was difficult. Her skin crawled and broke out in goose bumps as he seemed to look right inside her.

He pushed thinning strands of lank brown hair away from his damp forehead. "Well, aren't you going to get them out, then?"

"What?"

"Your books, Donna. Aren't you going to get them out of your bag?"

With trembling hands and cursing her nerves, Donna began to undo the fastenings at the top of her backpack. She tried not to feel Simon's steely eyes on her and just focused on pulling out the first book that her fingers touched.

Almost letting out the sigh of relief that threatened to burst through her chest, Donna gratefully looked down at an ancient copy of *Frenchman's Creek*.

"Got it," she said breathlessly. She hoped Simon wouldn't notice that the book didn't even belong on Quentin's shelves.

"Excellent." Simon rubbed his hands together so that the dry scraping sound they made was audible. Without another word he turned around and left the room.

Donna dropped Du Maurier's classic work of swash-buckling adventure and romance into her lap and brought shaking hands to her face. What had that been about? She knew there were secrets upon secrets in the Order—so much that she didn't know about, and probably never would—but Simon had just treated her like a criminal. He had been protecting the clock. But if it was such a big secret, why was it proudly on display in a public room? She'd been reading books in this library for most of her life. Then again, she had never really paid attention to the clock before. It was, after all, only a clock—something that was, as Simon himself had pointed out, just a piece of furniture.

As soon as she thought this, though, the answer came to her: *hiding in plain sight*. This was often the safest way to hide things, since the more important something was, the harder it became to find a foolproof hiding place. Why not just put it where everyone could see it, and where they would never even *imagine* there might be anything unusual?

Still trembling, Donna curled her legs beneath her and waited for her heart to stop pounding. She couldn't keep her gaze from wandering back to the tall grandfather clock. Her mind whirled with possibilities. What could be so important that the Order's secretary would yell at her just for laying a hand on it? The more she thought about it, the more she realized that the answers to all her questions might lie right here in the Blue Room—in Quentin's library.

If Simon Gaunt thought he'd succeeded in scaring her away from investigating further, he was making a big mistake.

Being brought up as a child of the alchemists pretty much sucks.

What makes it worse, though, in so many ways is that Mom and Dad are well-known and, even today, remembered as heroes—or so I'm told. The Underwood name is one to be reckoned with. Can you imagine the pressure that puts me under? Seriously, if I told everyone I just wanted to go to a regular college once I've graduated, maybe travel for a while and then study literature, or even take some courses in creative writing... yeah, my life wouldn't be worth living.

The Order has invested in me, you see. These tattoos of mine don't come cheap.

My childhood has been taken up with training, lessons, operations for my arms, and exercises to control my strength—an "unfortunate side effect" (Maker's words) of the iron holding me together.

It would be nice just to be a teenager.

But how is it fair that a teenager in the modern world should have to live by outdated rules laid down in dusty old books centuries ago? Rules made by a white, patriarchal system that patronized women and called them stupid things like "Moon Sister." Ugh.

Men like Quentin Frost. It's not like he's a bad person. I don't believe in things being that black or white; life is rarely that simple. Quentin is a kind enough guy, but that's just the point. Yet another old white dude telling us what's best for the alchemists and how they should survive in the New World.

Or men like his creepy partner, Simon. I honestly don't get what Quentin sees in him. I remember those two always being together, even before the attack in Ironwood Forest.

And then there's Maker, who I've always liked and trusted, but now... now I'm not so sure.

I want out so badly.

But, very occasionally, I wonder what my parents would think of that. Maybe I should stay and try to change things from the inside. Paige is fond of telling me that I'm one of the Next Generation—hope for the future of alchemy is in the hands of the young. As far as I'm aware, I'm the only person under the age of twenty-one from the Order of the Dragon. There are some younger Initiates in a couple of the other Orders, but for some reason ours is aging.

During my recovery—after Maker had branded me with iron and magic, and my arms were like broken wings lying useless and heavy on my bed—Quentin came to visit. I was back home by then.

(Our old home, closer to the Frost Estate and far-ther from the center of Ironbridge.) I didn't know Navin back then. I was eight years old, in con-stant pain, and all I could think about was Mom and Dad.

How could Patrick Underwood be dead?

What had happened to Rachel, his beautiful and talented wife?

I couldn't even comprehend those questions— let alone answer them—and yet there I was, left behind with an aunt I barely knew.

That was when Quentin started coming to Paige's little house, sitting next to me in the over-stuffed purple armchair and reading to me from books like Treasure Island, The Count of Monte Cristo, and Great Expectations. Books his father had read to him, that's what he told me. They were "boy's own" tales filled with adventure and hardship, and they showed me that there was a way to escape the pain—both physical and emo-tional—that I was going through.

He even introduced me to some of Mom's favorite novels, which launched my lifelong love of Daphne du Maurier. He would smile through his Santa Claus beard as he told me tales of pirates and smugglers and scary housekeepers. He had fewer lines on his face back then. A lot fewer.

I've never forgotten how kind Quentin was all those years ago.

But at the same time, I remember that Simon Gaunt never once came with him.

Eleven

Mildred's was a tiny coffee shop that stayed open from eight 'til eight most days. It was a favorite student haunt, but you could also find yourself rubbing shoulders with somber-suited office workers holding rushed meetings, juggling their laptops and lattes over the small tables. Nobody knew who Mildred actually was, or if indeed there had ever *been* a Mildred, but everyone who frequented the place was guaranteed a warm reception and the best cranberry muffins in New England.

Xan pushed open the brass-handled glass door and ushered Donna ahead of him. She was glad to be out of the cold, gratefully soaking up the atmosphere and warmth as well as the smell of coffee and pastries. While Xan placed their order, she made a beeline for the two-seater couch which was, miraculously, unoccupied. The rest of the coffee shop was full of people, most of whom had shopping bags crammed underneath their tables. She gratefully sank into the squashy brown velvet and wriggled out of her coat.

Her mind had been full of Simon's strange behavior all afternoon, but she'd had no trouble forgetting it as soon as it was finally time to leave the Frost Estate. She had a date to keep with the mysterious Mr. Grayson.

When Xan arrived, two steaming mugs and the muffins balanced precariously on a blue plastic tray, Donna again marveled at what was happening—at who she was hanging out with. She noticed two girls at a nearby table cast what they thought were surreptitious glances at her undeniably handsome companion, and then put their heads close together to whisper. *Kids*, she thought. And then had to smile at the irony. Wasn't she acting exactly the same way?

"So." Xan shrugged out of his coat and draped it over the back of the couch. "Cozy in this corner, isn't it?" He sat down next to her, his thigh almost touching hers as he made himself comfortable.

How did guys *do* that—manage to seem so at ease with themselves and the world around them? She still got so overwhelmed by things, and found it incredibly hard to hide her feelings. Aunt Paige had once accused her of "wearing her heart on her sleeve" too much, although Donna often wondered why that was such a bad thing.

Xan took a sip of his coffee. "I am so sorry about last night, what it must've looked like to you. The whole deal with the shirt." He shook his head with a wry grin. "I came across as pretty crazy."

"I sort of grew up with crazy, so it's okay." Donna broke little pieces off her muffin but didn't eat any. "I can't imagine what you must've gone through. How you … you know … lost what you did."

"You can't?" Xan's eyes glowed. "After what you showed me, I think you understand only too well."

She looked down at the table, not sure what to say next.

Xan reached out a tentative hand and touched the back of her emerald glove. When she'd pulled them on this morning before school, the color had reminded her of his eyes.

He cleared his throat, as though uncertain of something. "Can I see them again?"

She looked around the crowded café. "Here?"

"Here."

Donna surprised herself. Taking a deep breath, she turned to face Xan and, keeping her hands and arms low to hide them from the rest of the patrons, slowly peeled off the beautiful gloves and rolled up the sleeves of her sweater. She glanced nervously at the other people; she hadn't taken off her gloves in a public place for years. There was something so obviously *alien* about the markings that she was afraid of the reaction she might get. She certainly didn't want to have to start explaining them—nobody could possibly believe they were just regular tattoos.

But here, sitting next to her, was finally someone who knew something about the way she felt. Xan reached out and gently touched her wrist.

And then he winced and quickly pulled away.

"What happened?" Donna felt her eyes go wide.

Xan shrugged and half-smiled. "It's okay. I just didn't realize I could still be affected by iron. It's been so long."

Flushing, Donna tried to apologize, but the words stuck in her throat. I can't believe this, she thought. *I finally meet a guy I like and he's allergic to me.*

"It really is all right," said Xan, placing his hand over hers. "See? It was only for a moment—you must have pure iron in your hands. Star iron."

"Yeah, I'm practically glowing with the stuff." Donna couldn't keep the bitterness from her voice.

"I'm half-human, so I'm used to living in the iron world. It's just the 'hard stuff' I have a few problems with." He must have caught the anguished expression on her face because he suddenly grinned. "Hey, don't worry. They say opposites attract, right?"

Donna smiled, allowing herself to be reassured by his touch. She felt disappointed when he removed his hand.

"Do they hurt?" Xan asked.

"Not all the time," she admitted. "They ache sometimes, and I've been getting these shooting pains lately." She didn't tell him that those pains had been getting worse, especially each time she'd come into contact with the dark elves. "But it's a strange feeling, mostly. Like they're cold, so cold, in a bone-deep kind of way. It's like they'll never feel truly warm, you know?"

"They don't feel cold."

And then, as he reached out to touch the back of her hand once more, the markings shimmered more brightly and began to *move*, to curl and slide and slither along her flesh, sparkling under the overhead light.

Xan gasped and pulled back his hands. "What—"

Donna stared in shock. "That hasn't happened for years. I thought it had stopped." Her mind whirled with crazy thoughts. What the hell was happening? Was this part of the reason for the pain she'd been experiencing lately? Or was it something to do with Xan after all?

"They *move*," Xan whispered, awe radiating in his voice.

"Maker created them, so they have life in them. He works magically with metal. Iron and silver are his speciality, though, and he bonded the two together to, you know…fix me. Pure iron is soft and malleable." She looked at Xan, absurdly grateful to be talking to someone who understood this stuff without her having to explain every little thing. "You already know that the purest iron on our planet comes from space—"

"Right," he replied. "Meteorites."

"And then the silver was mixed with it, for its antibacterial qualities. Otherwise I might've died from iron poisoning when I was first tattooed."

Xan reached for her hands again and turned them palm-up. "There's hardly anything on your palms."

Donna nodded. "Never has been."

On the underside of her arms, the markings that began at the wrist were swirling up to the elbow crease. The movement gradually slowed down; the symbols lazily meandered along her skin as if deciding where and how to settle, what patterns to make. Donna was relieved for the dim lighting in this corner of the café, and she was mostly shielded from view by Xan as he moved closer to get a good look at her hands.

Picking up the discarded gloves, Donna began to pull them back on again. "Show's over." She tried to smile as she rolled the sleeves of her black sweater back down. Her jaw ached.

Xan pushed hair back from his face, his golden cheeks flushed with more than just the heat of his coffee. "Why do you hide them? You can see why I wouldn't want to advertise *my* scars. But yours? They're beautiful."

Shocked, Donna pulled away and tried to hide her hands. "They're not beautiful. Don't ever say that."

"Why not? This...Maker of yours has done an incredible job."

Tears pricked her eyes. "How can I possibly see something as beautiful when, every time I look at them...every single time...they remind me of what I've lost. Not just what happened to my hands, but to my family. To my parents."

Xan's expression was somber as he listened. He took a sip of his coffee and Donna couldn't help noticing that his hand trembled. "So, what happened to you?" he finally asked.

Donna took a deep breath and began to tell him the fairy-tale horror of her life. No Disney gloss for her; just the cold darkness of Grimm. "My parents belonged to the Order of the Dragon, an ancient alchemical secret society charged with many responsibilities, some of which I have no idea about. I don't even *want* to know, most of the time. Legend tells stories of the alchemists, but I can only tell you what *I* know. The Order has two main tasks: to guard the secret of immortality, and to protect humans from the otherworld. Which, of course, includes the inhabitants of Faerie."

Xan tucked one long leg under him, giving her all of his attention. "I know of the Order."

"Really? That's...unusual."

"You forget what I am."

"No." Her eyes locked with his. "No, I can never forget that."

He spoke as though he hadn't heard her. "You said your parents 'belonged' to the Order—past tense. What happened?"

"My father died protecting me from the wood elves when I was seven. My mother is in a secure medical facility. She was…damaged in some way. I don't know what happened to her; not exactly." Donna shook off his comforting hand. "Don't pity me, Xan, I can't stand it."

She took a slow, trembling breath. This was so much harder than she'd thought it would be. She usually tried hard to keep moving forward, to not dwell on the things she couldn't change, but meeting Xan had brought it all back again.

"Please," she said, desperation echoing in her voice. "Talk to me about something for a minute. Can you tell me about *your* parents?"

"All right." Xan shifted on the couch and rubbed his hands together. He looked nervous. "My father is from Faerie—a fey warrior of some kind. I never knew him, apart from what I found out years later. My human mother died in childbirth."

Donna tried to focus on *his* pain rather than her own, yet tears still threatened to break through at any moment. "Your father is still alive, then?"

"Perhaps. The faeries live long lives, though they are not quite immortal. For all I know, maybe he's not even aware I exist. He's no doubt living quite happily in Faerie, unhindered by a moment of weakness with a human woman." His eyes were far away.

Donna felt tired all of a sudden, as though a heavy weight was resting on her chest and her heart had turned to stone. "Xan, it's so hard, isn't it? Knowing these things. Having them be a part of our lives, but trying to pretend that everything is normal. Despite having Navin, I feel so alone. And then I feel guilty for even *thinking* that." She had so much else she wanted to say, but her throat felt tight and she couldn't continue.

"Guilty?" Xan leaned toward her. "For what?"

"For being disloyal to Navin, hiding so much from him over the years I've known him. We've shared a lot— lived next door to each other and spent so many evenings together. And how do I repay him? By lying to him the whole time we've known each other."

"Sometimes it's better to protect the ones you love."

"Said like a man who knows what he's talking about." Donna's voice held a lighter note, but it was forced and they both knew it.

"Well, I'm only talking from limited experience. My human parents adopted me despite my scars, but they obviously never knew what they were; what they meant about who and what I am. There are things about my life from before the adoption that even *I* can't face, let alone try to share them with anyone else." Xan stopped for a moment, letting the irony of his words hang in the charged air between them. He rushed on. "And, honestly? They didn't really care. I was just another possession to them, rather than a person they truly wanted."

Donna frowned. "A *possession*? What do you mean?" She couldn't imagine not being wanted. Even though her memories of life before the attack were vague, they were all happy. She knew she'd been loved by Patrick and Rachel Underwood, and that had kept her going through the long years of mourning and confusion.

"They were already rich when they adopted me, but they were pretty old—well, too old to easily adopt a baby even with all the money they had. Back then, the best they could do was a kid with scars and gaps in his memory. But I think they wanted to feel...*complete* as a family, you know? Like, having a child was the one thing they'd never done—never been *able* to do—so they wanted to be able to check that box."

"Xan, that's horrible. I'm so sorry."

He shrugged. "Hiding things from them became less important the older I got. They're busy people and both spend a lot of time overseas; since they got divorced it's been easier to just slip through the cracks. I've been emancipated from them since I was seventeen, anyway. My mother had won custody and she didn't fight me on it when I filed the petition—she's living back in England again. My father has let me live in the Ironbridge house ever since I dropped out of college."

Donna tried to imagine what Xan's life must have been like. She only knew a tiny part of his story, yet she felt her heart opening to him with each new revelation. There was something about Alexander Grayson that was both strong *and* vulnerable. Like he had the best reasons anyone could want if they were going to wallow in self-pity, but he refused to do that. He wore his sadness with dignity. It was refreshing, when you considered how the kids at Ironbridge High were so unbelievably emo with only the slightest provocation.

Silence rested between them, a delicate strand stretched shimmering tight. The sounds of other people around them drifted into background noise.

Donna was first to speak. "I think they close soon. The coffee shop, I mean."

Xan glanced at the display on his cell phone. "We've got a bit longer; there's still time for you tell me about your arms. What happened … when your father died?"

"I remember running through the woods, running from a pack of screeching elves. It's all so jumbled; I'm not even sure why I was there in the first place. Aunt Paige says I was taken by the elves, but…" She twisted her hands together and shrugged helplessly. "Honestly, Xan, I'm just not sure about any of it. I don't really understand why or how they'd be able to kidnap me from a house warded by alchemical magic."

"So what *do* you remember?"

"The sound," she replied. "The sound they made was *terrifying*. Some of the elves were riding on the back of a creature out of your worst nightmares, or maybe a horror movie—a giant black dog with yellow eyes and thick gray smoke for breath."

"A Skriker."

"Yes!" Realizing she'd raised her voice, Donna took a deep breath and spoke quietly. "Yes, that's it. I didn't know that until much later, of course. I researched the lore."

Xan nodded, a frown lining his brow. "The fey version of a hellhound. But isn't that a British legend?"

"Where do you think the fey came from in the first place? They're not natives of the United States, as far as I know." Donna smiled at the thought.

"I guess not." He shrugged. "So, is that how you were injured?"

Donna's lips trembled, but she pushed onwards. Surely it was good, telling someone who understood that strange and terrible world. "The Skriker attacked me, so I put my hands up to protect myself. When it bit me, it didn't feel like I thought teeth should, and I realized that its mouth was full of flames. But they were cold flames. So cold." Donna felt as though she were freezing in the warm café, and she became vaguely aware of Xan's arm around her. But she had to finish. She had to get through this.

With her voice lower than ever, she pushed on. "My hands and arms were frozen and burnt, all at the same time. The injuries were severe. Dad pulled me out of its jaws and made me run, despite the pain. There was no blood but it felt as though my arms were falling apart. He said the other alchemists were coming and that I could reach them if I just *kept running*. But I didn't go far. How could I leave him?" Her eyes filled with tears as she gazed blindly at Xan. "He died saving me."

Donna couldn't remember seeing her father fall, but she'd seen him afterwards—she was almost certain of it. There was an image that appeared in some of her dreams; a picture of Patrick Underwood lying in the Ironwood, as still and cold as the moon's reflection on the river. The frustrating thing, though, was that she only remembered snippets of that time, and many of the missing events had since been filled in by her aunt and other members of the Order. She was no longer quite sure what she genuinely recalled and which parts had been supplied for her by well-meaning adults.

"And that alchemist you talked about—Maker—he fixed your hands?" Xan asked quietly.

Donna took a shuddering breath. "Yes. He's an incredible man, with so much knowledge and power. I always get the impression he's been around for a lot longer than it seems."

Xan's green eyes shone brighter than ever. "Do you think he could do anything for me? I've always dreamed of finding a way to get my wings back."

"I...I don't know." She looked at him, feeling the first stirrings of excitement for him. A sudden image of the mechanical birds in the old alchemist's workshop filled her mind. "We could ask him, I guess." Though how she would explain this new friend to Maker, she had no idea. First Navin, now Xan. She wondered how much trouble she could possibly get into with the alchemists, but the hope on Xan's face was too much for her—she couldn't close down the possibility. At least, not yet.

"Xan," she said, pushing on before she could lose her nerve, "can you tell me ... how you lost your wings?"

"'Lost,' now that's an interesting choice of word." He laughed, a sound as joyless and unforgiving as a hard winter frost. "My wings were torn out of my back before they could even grow properly. Taken by the dark elves."

Donna felt the world around them stop. Some part of her had feared he might say this, and horror crept up her spine. "What happened?"

"After I was born, after my birth mother died, I was stolen from the hospital by fey beings and replaced with a changeling."

She could hardly take it in. "Wait a minute. You lived in Faerie?"

"No, I lived in the Elflands. I honestly don't remember much of my time there—and time moves differently in the sunless lands. I remember images, sounds ... it feels more like a dream." Xan seemed to be struggling under the weight of memory. "Or a nightmare."

He turned away from her, looking out the window and far into the distance.

Donna reached out and laid her hand over his; green satin on golden flesh. Nightmares were something she understood.

Xan cleared his throat but didn't move his hand away. "What I showed you last night—those scars on my back—that's a permanent reminder of my time with the elves. A reminder of my true heritage, and how it was stolen from me and I don't even know why."

"But you escaped."

He nodded. "And then I wandered into the arms of the authorities. Records were searched and national appeals went out, to try to track down any relatives of this strange boy who came out of the forest. There are press cuttings, you know … " His voice trailed off.

They both became aware of a waitress standing by their table. "I'm sorry, we're closing now." She held a tray filled with cups and plates and shifted from one foot to another. Emotion crackled in the air between Donna and Xan—it was a wonder the waitress's hair didn't fly with static.

They buttoned their coats and headed for the door.

Everyone else in the coffee shop seemed to have already left, but Donna couldn't remember any of it. She'd been so lost in her memories, and in Xan's own terrible story, that it had felt like being in a glass bubble. Walking out into the freezing air should have been a cruel wake-up call, but despite her sadness there was still an ember of warmth in her chest that glowed each time she looked at her companion.

She smiled as Xan reached down and took her hand in his.

This time he walked her all the way home.

When Donna turned up the walk to her aunt's house, she didn't get very far. Xan was still holding on to her.

"What's wrong?" She examined his face with concern.

His lips quirked and she had the feeling he might be teasing her. "Didn't you forget something?" he asked.

Donna frowned. "Um, I don't think so?" She hadn't meant to make it a question, but the growing smile that played across his mouth had gotten her all hot and confused. It was a relief to see him smiling again, after what they'd shared at Mildred's.

His fingers were still curled lightly around her wrist. She glanced down as he tugged her toward him, and she took a couple of stumbling steps forward. Her free hand came up to brace herself against his chest. Her heart was pounding so hard she thought she could feel the echo all the way down to her toes. All she could see were Xan's eyes—they looked otherworldly as they glittered under the streetlight.

He kissed her then, not giving her a chance to say anything or to pull away. His warm hands moved to cup her face as he guided her mouth right to where he wanted it.

She felt weak and sort of boneless, and all she could focus on was the feel of Xan's lips on hers; the way they moved with a perfect combination of gentle warmth and insistent pressure. He tasted vaguely of pears, with a hint of tobacco. Donna wished she knew if she was doing it right, but it wasn't exactly the sort of thing you could just *ask*. She was lightheaded and dizzy, but in the best possible way—in a way that she never wanted to end.

But it did end. Eventually Xan pulled away, and she opened her eyes to find him watching her. The smile had returned to his face, but it was a *good* smile, a happy smile.

She didn't know if she would be able to talk, not after that. Maybe not ever again.

"Wow." Okay, so she could talk—but she hadn't meant to say that out loud.

Xan's laugh was shaky, stripped of all self-confidence. "Yeah. That sums it up pretty well."

Donna wished he would kiss her again. Of course, she could kiss *him*, but the thought made her stomach flip over. Probably better to get inside while she could still walk straight.

She tried a smile. "Good night. Thanks for…you know…for talking."

"You too," he replied softly. "I'll call you tomorrow."

Heading into the house as fast as she could, Donna wondered how on earth she was going to get through the rest of the night. Not just because of Xan, but because of what had happened at the Frost Estate with Simon Gaunt. Everything was strange and confusing, and she wasn't sure *what* to think right now.

And then there was Navin. Her relationship with him was in a delicate place and, just because he *appeared* to be adjusting to this whole new level of crazy, that didn't mean things would run smoothly from here on out.

When she finally managed to fall sleep, the shadows returned darker than ever to plague her dreams.

She was standing in a room full of grandfather clocks, all chiming midnight in a chorus of mournful sound—and over the ringing of the hollow chimes she could hear somebody calling her name, screaming for help. But the clocks were so noisy that she couldn't make out who needed her, and every time she tried to leave the room, she was faced with yet another clock standing in her way. Every path was blocked.

The blue walls were lined with bookshelves—bookshelves on every wall—and they were overflowing with enough reading material to last several lifetimes. But she couldn't move a single one of them. No matter how many books she attempted to open and how hard she tried, she couldn't see inside because each one had been nailed shut.

Simon sat on a navy velvet couch watching her, and Maker had his back turned while he bent to examine the front of one of the clocks. When Donna touched him on the shoulder he turned slowly to look at her—only his eyes were blank spaces and his teeth were too sharp.

Twelve

Donna checked her phone for what seemed like the hundredth time since she'd gotten up. Still nothing from Navin, and she hadn't seen any sign of movement next door. Even when she'd woken from one of the dreams and looked out of her bedroom window in the early hours, something about the Sharmas' place seemed...empty.

It was unusual for Navin not to reply to her text messages or return her calls. She'd tried to contact him before falling into bed last night. Several times.

Donna let herself out of the house and carefully locked the door behind her, trying not to let thoughts of Xan take over her brain for the day. Just remembering that kiss from last night made her toes curl. Seeing him again couldn't come soon enough, yet she was still sort of nervous about it. She shook her head and made a valiant attempt to focus on other things.

Aunt Paige had left for work at seven-thirty as usual, leaving Donna to make her own way to the estate for her lessons. Today she was due to work on practical exercises with Quentin, one of those rare occasions when the arch-master of the Order personally shared his knowledge with a potential initiate. It was not something she was looking forward to—especially after what had happened yesterday. But maybe Simon hadn't snitched. *Yeah, right.*

Cutting her eyes across to the Sharmas' front door, she decided to give it one last try before heading off. She was already in danger of being late, but she couldn't get Navin's silence out of her mind. Of course, there was that time his cell phone was stolen and she'd tried to ring him for hours while he was stuck filling out reports with the police. But what were the chances it would've happened again?

When Nisha yanked open the door, seconds after she'd rung the bell, Donna almost jumped out of her skin.

"Nisha! You're home!"

The girl flicked long hair over her shoulder with one hand, furiously brushing her teeth with the other. She nodded and removed the toothbrush from her mouth, speaking around bubbles of white foam. "Mmm. Grandfather was ill yesterday so we went to visit and ended up staying pretty late. He's okay now, though."

Donna barely registered the news that their grandfather was better, simply feeling her entire body sag with relief that there was an explanation for Navin's disappearance. "So all of you went? Navin, too?"

"Uh-huh. You only just missed him. He left for school a minute ago. You might be able to catch him at the bus stop if you make a run for it."

Donna immediately frowned. "Why is *Navin* taking the *bus*?"

Nisha rolled her eyes. "Oh, I don't know. Something's wrong with his bike. He was really moody about it." She glanced at the pink watch on her slim brown wrist and pulled a face around her mouthful of toothpaste. "I'm running late, Donna, better go."

"Sure, sorry. I'll let you go. Thanks, Nisha."

Navin's sister closed the door, returning to tooth-brushing and whatever else she had to do before a busy day of preening and posing at Ironbridge High.

Holding her messenger bag to keep it from banging against her hip, Donna ran back down the street, turning left at the corner and heading toward the bus stop at the end of the next road. Her black sequinned sneakers pounded the sidewalk. She tried to focus all her energy on reaching the next street in time to see Navin before they were separated by school for the day. Perhaps, she told herself, he'd lost his phone in all the worry over his grandfather; that would explain why he hadn't responded to any of her messages.

Donna didn't want to think about the possibility that Navin might have had second thoughts about their friendship. Maybe he wasn't adjusting as well as she'd hoped.

She ran around the bend, almost knocking over a bag-laden mother pushing a stroller. She spotted the bus stop and the green city bus approaching it at the same moment. Desperately scanning the short line of people waiting by the shelter, she thought she saw Navin's black and red jacket. Donna forced a last burst of speed from her pumping legs, gasping for breath and trying to ignore the heavy bag bashing against her back.

"Navin!" she yelled, still halfway down the road. "Nav, wait!"

It was definitely Navin; Donna watched as he stepped onto the bus and showed his pass to the driver. Still running, she felt panic welling up inside her like a cold spring. She had a sharp unpleasant taste in her mouth, and didn't know if it was from the running or the thought of missing Navin.

She reached the bus stop just as the bus was pulling away. Jumping onto the scarred wooden bench of the bus shelter, she tried to catch a glimpse of Navin's dark hair or eye-catching jacket. She was rewarded when the bus had to slow down for a foolish driver who'd swung out of a parking space into its path.

Practically flying off the bench and running down the sidewalk in pace with the crawling bus, Donna briefly hoped someone inside would tell the driver to stop, thinking she'd missed it. If she could just locate Navin, get his attention ... just one glance, one moment of eye contact ...

And then, through one of the dusty windows toward the middle of the bus, she saw him. Navin's head was leaning against the glass; he had headphones on and was nodding in time to the music. She cast a desperate glance at the obstructing car, which was now doing a U-turn in the middle of the street, and felt grateful for a serendipitous moment of bad driving.

"Navin!" she shouted, knowing even as she did so that it was useless. Frustration gripped her as she stepped into the street, cutting between precariously parked cars to reach Navin's window. *Please, Navin*, she thought. She considered trying his phone again, but then the bus roared its throaty engine, preparing to accelerate.

"Crap."

At that moment, the pale morning sun hit the window at a particular angle, momentarily cutting through the dust and grime and giving her a gloriously clear view into the bus. She fixed her eyes on Navin, willing him to turn and look out the window. Couldn't he sense her there? What was *wrong* with him?

Fingers of sunlight touched his cheek ... blue highlights flashed in his ebony hair ... and then Donna saw *right through him*. One moment he was just Navin, sitting real and solid against the window. The next moment he was like a hollow ghost, a physical shell around a black and twisted shadow, creeping vines and bony shoulders, gnarled fingers holding on to the seat in front as the bus leapt forwards.

Donna fell backwards as the bus moved away in a cloud of exhaust, holding her hand to her mouth in shock. "Oh my God, oh my God," she repeated over and over, like a mantra. "Oh please, no. No, no, no."

As she stood in the wake of the departing bus, frozen in shock and terror, she tried to convince herself that what she'd just witnessed had been a trick of the light. Perhaps she'd been blinded by the sunlight reflected on the windowpane.

But even as these thoughts piled on top of more and more desperate attempts at rationalization, she knew she was fighting a losing battle. The churning pain in her gut told her that she hadn't made a mistake. She'd glimpsed the true form of the thing sitting on the bus—in Navin's place.

With so much metal around to distract and distort the elf's magic, its elfskin was precarious. It was difficult for it to uphold a convincing disguise. But this elf had made an almost foolproof stab at it, until that sliver of light had fallen *just so*, enabling Donna to make the leap required to really see. It must be an incredibly strong creature to be able to keep its glamour while sitting on a steel-encased bus.

How was it even possible? And what was it doing? Was it actually going to go to school in Navin's place?

Realizing she was still standing in the road, Donna stepped onto the sidewalk and slowly walked back to the bus stop. She still had to get her own bus to Quentin's, but how was she supposed to concentrate on studying? Sitting down on the bench, gnawing at her bottom lip, Donna wondered whether she could get out of her lessons.

Navin was gone. She almost whimpered as she allowed the reality to sink in. What was she going to do? As soon as she gave that plaintive thought a voice, she knew it sounded pathetic, but she really couldn't help it. And then that stronger part of her spoke up—the voice she liked to think of as her father's: *You'll find him, Donna. You will find out what happened to him and bring him home.*

And Maker, too.

Of course! She wanted to smack herself over the head for being so dumb. Maybe Maker had seemed strange on Sunday because…well, because it hadn't really been Maker at all. Everything was becoming clear, and a whole new bunch of questions were popping up in desperate need of answers.

Donna knew she needed to first deal with the immediate problem—Alma Kensington was waiting for her at the Frost Estate. She punched the familiar keys on her cell phone and waited to be connected directly to her tutor.

"Kensington," came the clipped tones.

"Alma, it's Donna."

"Donna, is everything all right?"

"Actually, no. I'm afraid I don't feel very well. I got as far as the bus stop—in fact, I'm still here—but I've got a terrible headache and I feel really dizzy."

"Do you feel well enough to get back home again?" Genuine concern peeked through Alma's usually business-like voice, but Donna only allowed herself to feel a little guilty for lying.

"It's not far, thanks. I can manage."

"Well, it's better to be careful, especially when you're traveling. I'll call your aunt at work and let her know."

Great, now Aunt Paige would worry. Donna hoped her aunt wouldn't get the urge to stop in at lunchtime to check on her. She turned and walked back toward the house, not intending to stick around there playing the invalid. She needed to make a plan. Mostly, she needed to figure out how on earth the wood elves had become strong enough to infiltrate the city.

And most important of all: why was one walking around Ironbridge masquerading as Navin Sharma?

Thirteen

Lying motionless on her bed, eyes closed in concentration, Donna's first impulse was to go to Maker's workshop to see if he was still acting strangely. If he was, well...she was increasingly certain that she knew why. It seemed Navin wasn't the only one with a doppelganger walking around in his place.

The thought filled Donna with dread, but this would explain the subtle quirks in Maker's recent behavior, the nagging feeling she'd had that something was just a little bit *off*. And then there was the pain in her hands—she'd attributed it to the wood elf in the bathroom, but now that she thought about it, the sensation had started up again while she was standing with the old alchemist outside the workshop.

It was almost as though the iron in her hands and arms was reacting to fey magic.

She shivered. Perhaps going to the workshop alone wasn't such a good idea. It was too quiet there, too hidden away, with a potential for attack.

Pushing herself up off the bed, Donna squared her shoulders and made a decision. She would get a cab to Ironbridge High and see if there was any sign of "Navin" at school. Perhaps the elf would show up for homeroom and then leave. If that was the case, she might be in time to catch up with it—maybe even follow the thing.

If she had to, she would confront it.

Navin—the *real* Navin—needed her. Donna would do whatever it took to get him back.

Standing outside the gates of Ironbridge High, Donna experienced a rush of nerves that threatened to melt her resolve. The school was the site of many painful memories. She certainly didn't relish being anywhere near it, yet now here she was, contemplating walking through those gates to search for Navin. But she would do *anything* for him, and walking into a place that had become like hell on earth for her was nothing compared to the possibility of losing Nav.

The first period of classes had already started, so Donna was able to walk to the main office without having to speak to anyone who knew her. She kept her head down, just in case, moving quickly and with a sense of purpose she didn't feel.

The office was the same bustling, friendly place it had always been. Through the large window at the counter, she could see two women juggling piles of paper, and she recognized one of her old teachers battling with the photocopier behind them. Donna hoped he wouldn't recognize her voice; she wasn't in the mood to have a polite conversation with Mr. Jackson about how she was doing. Then one of the receptionists looked up from her filing and smiled.

"Oh, hello dear. Didn't you ring the bell?" The middle-aged woman approached the window and slid the hatch wider. She had a round face, with lines that crinkled the corners of her eyes in a way that made Donna feel more at ease.

"I only just got here," Donna said. "I'm still a student, but I'm mostly home-schooled now. I do my exams here."

"Can I see your I.D.?"

Donna pulled out her laminated pass, giving a barely audible sigh of relief when the woman glanced at it and nodded.

"I'm waiting for my friend to finish his class. We're attending an appointment together and he's late."

"What's his name?"

"Navin Sharma. He's a senior."

The woman went over to a computer terminal and started tapping on the keys, squinting as she followed the information on the screen.

Donna tried not to show her impatience, but, nice as the receptionist was, she was taking her sweet time. Couldn't she tell how important this was? Just as Donna was seriously contemplating putting her fist through the window, climbing across the counter, and pushing the woman out the way so she could look up Nav's schedule herself, the receptionist turned and walked slowly back to the window.

"He'll be with Mrs. Kramer, I think. Room 203. Wait, you need a hall pass—"

Screw the hall pass, Donna thought savagely, racing to the north stairwell and up to the second floor in the oldest wing of the school. There were only five more minutes until morning break.

She crept as close to the door of Room 203 as she dared and peered through the criss-cross pattern stamped onto the glass window, doing her best to think invisible thoughts. If anyone saw her standing out here, she was just going to hope that the floor would swallow her up. Melanie Swan would most likely be in this class with Nav, and that was one confrontation she could do without.

Scanning the heads of the students bent over text-books and hoping that Mrs. Kramer wouldn't notice her, Donna almost shouted with relief when she saw the back of Navin's head and his bony shoulder blades poking through his white T-shirt. His ever-present jacket was slung across the back of his chair. Then she had to remind herself that it *wasn't* Navin. Although it might be just as well to check before leaping on him and yelling "elf."

Heart pounding, Donna stepped back from the window and waited in the corridor, wondering what on earth she was supposed to do now. The "enemy" was right there, sitting in a *school classroom* as though it didn't have a care in the freaking world. Just for a second, Donna considered barging into the Mayor's office and telling Aunt Paige everything; but how could she explain why she hadn't said anything before? Sure, Maker—if it really *was* Maker—had encouraged her to keep quiet about what happened at his place, but what about the next day? On Monday she and Xan had been attacked by a stray on Ironbridge Common, yet she'd chosen to keep it a secret.

But she hadn't wanted to tell Aunt Paige about Xan, and it was one of those situations that had just gained momentum on its own—Donna never would have guessed that an unplanned visit to Maker and the appearance of a lone dark elf in the city would have set all these events in motion. Sometimes the longer you left something without telling people, the harder it got to open your mouth and start filling them in on what they'd missed. She'd learned that the hard way after three years of keeping secrets from Navin. And of course, if she talked to Aunt Paige, her aunt would talk to the Order. Donna was convinced that this wasn't the best idea.

The school bell rang, making her heart pound harder than ever. Glad that her palms didn't sweat, she still reflexively rubbed her gloved hands against her jeans. She licked her dry lips and listened to the manic activity that had sprung up all around her. Chairs scraped back, doors opened and closed, and footsteps that were more like a herd of elephants clumped up and down the stairs.

Then the door to Mrs. Kramer's classroom opened and students poured out in a steady stream of chatter. Donna had positioned herself just to the left of the doorway, her back to the wall, hoping that the majority of her ex-classmates would head in the opposite direction, toward the stairwell. She kept alert, waiting for the thing masquerading as Navin to leave the room.

Luckily, only a handful of students noticed her; they promptly turned their heads as if they'd just seen a mirage. That was fine by her. But it looked like her luck had run out when Melanie Swan's glossy hair swung past. Turning the other way down the hall, away from the crowd of students, Melanie swept right by Donna, almost touching her. Then she did a double-take. It would have been funny if Donna had had the time to appreciate it.

"Underwood, what are you doing here? Are there *special* exams today?" A couple of Melanie's hangers-on giggled.

"I don't have time for you," Donna replied calmly, looking around Melanie's head and keeping her eyes trained on the door.

"Ah, waiting for your *boyfriend*, are we?"

"Melanie, don't mess with me. I'm really not in the mood."

"Oh *really*, is it that time of the month, freak? I didn't think you'd even started yet." Melanie laughed at her own joke, hands resting on her narrow hips as she pulled herself up to her full, willowy height.

A small crowd was beginning to gather around them as Donna saw the Navin-clone walk out of the classroom and head toward the stairs.

"Sorry, Mel, I've got more important things to do." She pushed past the sneering girl and ducked between two other students, preparing to follow her only lead in finding Navin.

A hand grabbed her shoulder and pulled her backwards, causing her to stumble. Righting herself and whipping around, Donna came nose to nose with Melanie.

"We're not finished here yet, Underwood."

She couldn't believe that Melanie Swan had actually laid hands on her. The girl's cronies were watching eagerly, scenting an exciting interlude in their day, and a couple of other random students were loitering nearby. Trying to keep her already frayed temper in check, Donna glanced behind her, knowing that every second that passed took Navin farther away from her.

"I told you, I don't have time for this bullshit." Donna enunciated every word clearly. She turned to walk away, furious that a couple of the kids actually sighed with disappointment at the thought they might not get the fight they were hoping for.

"You're not getting away this time, *freak*," Melanie said. "Your little boyfriend isn't here to protect you now."

"I don't need anyone to protect me," Donna said as scathingly as she could. "Or have you forgotten?"

"Ooh, listen to her," mocked Melanie. She reached out and grabbed the lapel of Donna's jacket.

Instinct took over. Donna laid her gloved hand over Melanie's wrist and squeezed, gently to begin with, then slowly forcing the hand to unlock from her jacket. She felt the power of her grip, pure steel wrapped in a sheath of satin.

"Ow, get off me!" Melanie shrieked, all the confidence draining out of her in a rush of intense pain.

Looking the girl in the eye, Donna kept hold of her wrist and continued to push her backwards, squeezing more tightly and all the while keeping a fixed smile on her face. "Don't you ever lay hands on me again, *Mel*," she said quietly.

Melanie Swan whimpered and tried to pry Donna's hand away from her wrist, but there was no shaking the iron grip. Tears filled Melanie's eyes; the other students started to mutter and look at Donna with fear. She'd seen those looks before, but this time the shame didn't weigh so heavily on her.

Releasing Melanie's arm, she turned and walked toward the stairwell, shoulders pulled back and head held high. She heard Melanie's concerned friends and the other onlookers clustering around her, making sympathetic noises, and she tried to feel remorse for what she'd done.

But searching inside, all Donna could feel was a cold, hard fury. There was no way she could catch up to that creature now.

She had as good as lost Navin.

Fourteen

Ttrying to swallow her anger and disappointment, Donna walked up and down the street outside Ironbridge High. There was a bitter taste in her mouth that she couldn't get rid of.

The day stretched ahead of her, unfilled hours where she could be *doing* something to find Nav. Tugging her cell phone out of her jeans pocket, she dialed and waited, still pacing back and forth in front of the school railings.

"Yes?"

"Xan, it's Donna."

"I know." She heard the smile in his lazy voice and tried to ignore the warm feeling spreading through her chest.

"Xan, I need your help." There, she'd said it. She couldn't go back now.

"What can I do?" No hesitation in his voice, just a steady certainty that he was there for her.

Donna closed her eyes for a moment, allowing herself to bask in the feeling that she wasn't alone, even with Navin gone. "My friend Navin is in trouble and I have to find him. I was following the thing that might be able to lead me to him, but I lost it."

"'Thing'? I assume we're not talking about a person."

She gave a shaky laugh. "No, obviously not. Look, Xan…this could get dangerous. You don't have to do it."

"I don't even know what I have to do yet, do I?"

"I'm sorry, I'm not making any sense. I need—"

His reassuring voice cut her off. "Where do you want me to meet you?"

Overwhelmed with relief, Donna told him where she was and settled in to wait.

He arrived in a sturdy-looking Volvo. Its faded crimson bodywork shone in the thin sunlight, and the various dents and rust spots made it look sort of homey and familiar. Donna had never wanted to learn to drive a car (what with the whole super-strength-kicking-in-under-pressure thing), but she could picture learning in this one. Maybe with Xan sitting by her side and patiently coaching her on how to handle a stick.

She had to shake herself out of the daydream and concentrate on the very real emergency they faced.

Xan listened patiently while the words tumbled out of her mouth. She told him of her new suspicions about Maker, and filled him in on Navin's doppelganger and how she'd seen through its glamour on the bus. She knew Xan was probably most concerned about Maker, given his hopes of getting help from the old alchemist in the future, but he was careful not to focus on that. He took everything in stride.

But then, what had she expected? After what he'd been through in his own life—and what he *was*—he surely was already her friend, even though they'd only met three days ago. And to be honest, she knew they were more than friends now. Not just because of the awful truths they'd shared, but because of what had happened on the way home last night. Donna thought of the kiss and her stomach tightened.

Xan hadn't kissed her yet today. After he'd parked the car (which his father had been intending to scrap, he said), he'd swept her into a bone-crushing hug and then just set her away from him and looked at her.

"Is there anything you can do?" Donna asked. They were standing across from the school, leaning against the red brick wall of an old apartment building as the sun moved slowly above them in a surprisingly blue sky. She was trying not to sound as desperate as she felt, but she didn't think she was doing too good a job of it. Her eyes kept burning with unshed tears, and then she'd feel irritated with herself for letting her worries get the better of her. She needed to focus if she was going to find out what had happened to Navin; she rubbed a hand across her face. "Could you maybe, I dunno ... track the wood elf, somehow? That's why I wanted you to come here—this is where I last saw it."

Xan looked doubtful. "I don't know, Donna. Any real magic I might have had—or *should* have had—got totally messed up after they took my wings. I'm only half faery. I can do a few things, but they're not much more than pretty tricks."

She let out a frustrated breath, temporarily pushing aside her curiosity about what "pretty tricks" he might be able to do. "But there must be *something* we can try. I can't just let it go like this. That creature was right *here*."

He looked at her with the lazy green eyes that made her heart beat faster. "There is something, but I don't know if it will work. It's been a long time since I tried to find one of the Old Paths."

Donna's eyes lit up. "You know how to get into the *Elflands*?"

"Don't get too excited. I used to know. I'm not sure any more, but it might be worth a try." Xan's eyes clouded for a moment, as if trying to capture a memory. "When

I was younger—after I was first adopted—I had a lot of dreams. Dreams about the wood elves and what they did to me. It was all just a confused mess. My adoptive parents had me seeing a child psychologist by this time, and I was encouraged to think of the dreams as symbolic. Not actual events."

Donna touched his arm. "But they were. Real, I mean."

"Yeah. And one of the recurring dreams is of me running out of the Ironwood, following a path I'd seen the elves walk many times before while they held me captive."

"One of the Old Paths," Donna breathed, trying to control her mounting excitement. She was surprised to find her thoughts wandering toward her aunt and the Order. If *they* knew how to get into the Elflands, it could mean an end to the standoff that had been in place for so many years. The alchemists could drive the wood elves out once and for all.

Xan's lips thinned. "I can see what you're thinking, but I'm really not sure my memory is reliable. And you must know that any sort of door to *any* faery realm, even a temporary home here in our world, will be protected. The doors move, too, once they're discovered. One door could be in a hundred different places, depending on the day. We just have to hope that the one I know of is still there—it could be, if it's been untouched for the past decade or so."

Donna nodded. "It's okay; I'm not planning on riding into battle against the wood elves quite yet. I just want to find Navin. And Maker."

"If they've got him as well."

"I'm certain of it." And she was. "Nav's my best friend, Xan. I just can't imagine a day going by where I don't speak to him. I have to find him. It's selfish of me, I know that."

He shook his head slowly. "No, no, I understand. I lost a friend like that. Our friendship was the only reason I know anything concrete about my past." Xan swallowed. "It just happened last year."

"Oh my God, I'm so sorry." Donna laid a hand on his arm, feeling sadness burning in the center of her chest.

He shook off her hand, his jaw tightening as he stared straight ahead. "I couldn't change things, and I *should* have been able to."

She didn't know what to do. "I'm sorry," she repeated, feeling miserable and useless.

Xan shoved his hands into his coat pockets, his shoulders slumped. Donna could only guess at how much this must be costing him, and she wondered at his willingness to come back into contact with the dark elves. She knew it was because of her—he was doing it *for* her—but she didn't know what to do with that knowledge. She bit her lip, thinking she should apologize again.

"Forget it," he said, his voice unbearably grim. "I guess we're heading into the Ironwood."

They took the most direct route out of the city and parked just a short walk from the dark green Ironwood. It was lunchtime, and the late autumn sun had climbed high above them; it warmed Donna's face despite the chill in the air. She closed her eyes for a delicious moment.

"Come on, I don't think you're going to catch much of a tan out here." Xan raised a golden eyebrow.

She shrugged. "I know that. It's just so beautiful. I love autumn and winter—I always have. Don't you think there's something magnificent about it?"

"It's magnificently cold, is what it is. Let's get moving." He turned and strode toward the woodland.

Donna sighed and ran a few steps to catch up.

The low fence surrounding the trees was old and rotten in places, as though there hadn't been any maintenance in a long time. Just outside of it was a row of sturdy iron streetlights encircling the whole woodland like sentries—a steel fortification designed to create a prison of what remained of the Elflands.

Donna followed Xan through the gateway marking the entrance, glancing back at the traffic passing by on the main road. It felt a little bit like walking out of one world and into another. The leaf and needle strewn pathway opened up ahead of them, under a varied canopy of wintering branches and evergreens.

It was much quieter in here. The sounds of the road were muffled behind the tree trunks, and all of a sudden seemed very far away. Donna took a deep breath, momentarily forgetting what they were supposed to be doing and just enjoying the freshness and fragrant smells of the woods. She was soon snapped back to reality.

"We have to go further in," Xan said. "I'll know it if we get near the Old Path."

She touched his arm. "Wait a second. How will you know?"

"I honestly have no idea. It's like there's something in my chest, sort of tugging me toward it. I can't explain it any better than that."

"Like a magnet?"

"Yeah, something like that." Xan shook his head, clearly frustrated and not liking the fact that he had to rely on something out of his control.

They walked in silence for a while. Donna listened to the sounds of the wildlife, wondering how the place that featured so strongly in her nightmares could seem almost beautiful now that she was actually in it again. It had been ten long years since she'd set foot beneath these trees. She repressed a shiver and pulled her thin jacket more tightly around her.

She wished that Xan would hold her hand like he had last night, but he seemed lost in his own thoughts.

Leaves and branches crackled underfoot. It grew darker as they walked farther and deeper along the straight path. Despite the fall of leaves, the evergreens were plenty big enough to blot out the blue sky. The sun could only be seen in slivers of yellow light falling briefly between the trees before disappearing, only to reappear for a moment in another shadowed gap.

Donna slowed her pace and frowned. "Look, the path splits off here. Which way do we go?"

Xan walked to the miniature crossroads, resting his hand on the trunk of an old oak and closing his eyes. Donna watched him, trying not to think about how his hair fell onto his forehead and made him look younger than his nineteen years. She suddenly thought of Navin and what might be happening to him, but she tried not to be impatient. She refused to believe Navin was anything other than alive and well—they just had to find him, and then everything would be all right.

Xan opened his eyes and nodded toward the right-hand pathway. "This way."

"Are you sure?"

He shrugged. "Not really, but it's the best we've got." He glanced at her. "Don't you remember *any* of this?"

"No, I told you, I hardly remember anything." Donna swallowed as she thought of her father. "My dreams show me a clearing, every single time, but I don't know if it's real or imagined."

He took her hand in his. Her glove sitting in his large hand made her feel warm and safe. "Maybe we'll find out," he said.

Trying to smile, Donna gently squeezed his fingers, ignoring the memory of what she'd done to Melanie earlier. Sometimes the strength in her hands scared her, but it seemed that she only did the *really* crazy-powerful stuff when her emotions and adrenaline were running high.

Xan looked into her eyes. "Donna, I'm so glad I found you."

Her breath caught in her throat. "Hey," she said, trying to keep her voice light. "*I* found *you*, don't forget."

"I'm glad you could look beyond how stupid I acted that night up on the roof. I behaved like an idiot."

"No you didn't." Well, she thought, maybe a little. She bit her lip to keep from smiling.

"I did, and we both know it. I was showing off—hiding behind some kind of mysterious face that isn't really me at all." He grinned. "Not all the time, anyway."

They followed the path to the right, walking in silence again. Donna found her thoughts straying to Quentin's grandfather clock. Maybe she could get another look at it tomorrow, when she went back to her classes with Alma.

And then she stopped walking, brought up short by Xan, who had paused in front of her. He was staring off into the undergrowth on the left of the pathway, his eyes taking on a haunted look that left her breathless with fear.

"Xan, what is it?" She stepped forward, wondering whether she should touch him or not. He seemed turned to stone, his jaw clenching and his usually golden skin pale in the dim light slipping through the trees.

"We're here."

Donna looked around, wondering how on earth he could tell. All the trees looked the same to her, although the undergrowth seemed to crowd closer and there was less light here. Xan was staring into the depths of the trees, toward a clump of long-leafed bushes. There didn't appear to be anything unusual about it to Donna.

At least, not to start with. But when her hands started to throb and the familiar ache started up in her wrists and arms, she began to suspect that they were in the right place after all.

Xan cleared his throat. "We need to go through there." He reached for her hand again and she gratefully clasped it in her own. "Donna, are you sure you want to do this?"

She nodded. "Absolutely." Her stomach tightened, but she knew she had no choice. She had to go after Navin.

Xan stepped off the path, taking her with him. They began to work their way through the tangled undergrowth, ducking beneath branches and vines that reached out for them and brushed their faces. Donna tried to ignore the steady ache in her hands, hanging onto Xan and concentrating on making sure she didn't get a stray branch in her eye.

Pushing his way between two towering, dark green bushes, Xan bent the brambles out of Donna's way so she could duck underneath his arm and slip through the gap. The eerie silence made her heart beat so loudly she wondered if he could hear it.

And then, on the other side of the spiteful branches, Donna found herself standing in a tiny clearing. Not the clearing of her dreams—no, this one provided barely enough space for the two of them to stand, together, on the dead leaves that littered the ground. Tree trunks pressed in all sides, the moss-covered bark smelling musty and vaguely rotten.

Even without her history with the alchemists, Donna would have known she was in a magical place—and it wasn't a benign sort of magic, either. There was an oppressive feel that didn't just come from the crowded trees. The air was full of a dull heaviness that weighed on her shoulders and made it difficult to breathe properly. She glanced at Xan to see if he felt it too.

He raised his eyebrows. "Are you okay?"

She shook her head. "Don't you feel that?"

"We're approaching the doorway—the elves' power is at its strongest here. That's probably what you're picking up on."

"But you don't feel that... *weight* on you?"

"I have fey blood, don't forget. I can feel a sort of energy—a buzz all around me—but it doesn't feel all that bad."

Donna felt a shiver run through her. Xan's eyes seemed greener than ever; they burned with a deep emerald fire, confirming that he wasn't fully human. She took a deep breath. "So, what now?"

"This is it." His voice was steady—all the uncertainty he had earlier seemed to have left him. Clearly he was being led by something other than dream or memory. A knowledge that ran bone-deep guided them both, now.

"But…there's nothing here." Donna looked around, wondering if she'd missed something.

"Not yet," replied Xan. He crouched down on the ground and ran his hands over the dark earth. He grabbed a handful of dirt and leaves and a few twigs, then stood and faced her once more. "Put your hand on mine so that you're touching this stuff."

Donna did as she was told. "What are you doing?"

"Opening the door." Xan closed his eyes for a moment. Donna was almost certain she could see a glow escaping from beneath his lids, but he re-opened his eyes before she could be sure. "I was lucky enough to find someone, eventually—a mentor who guided me through the basics of this stuff, taught me about my heritage."

"I'd like to hear about him someday."

"*Her*," replied Xan. "She was a good friend."

Donna determinedly ignored the stab of jealousy she felt. Now wasn't the time to act like a child. Xan's mentor being female didn't mean anything.

His eyes softened as he watched her. "She's the friend who died last year."

Oh. Way to feel like a totally heartless bitch. "Xan, I—"

He shook his head. "Not now," he said. "I need to focus."

And then Donna forgot about everything. Her eyes widened as she watched Xan become more ethereal, less solid. There was a translucent quality to his golden skin, and she felt a rush of heat against her face. The blast of hot air seemed to be coming from ... *Xan*. So here was the guy who couldn't do fey magic, apart from "pretty tricks." *Riiight*.

He spoke. "We seek the Old Path and approach the door. I hold earth in my hand and invoke the power in my blood—the blood of my ancestors. I ask to be granted entrance to this dark place. We come in peace. Open!"

Donna jumped as he shouted the last word, but she kept her grip on the bundle of dirt and leaves that they held. The air in front of her seemed to shimmer and thicken, and for a moment darkness folded itself around her. It was a peculiar kind of blackness, with a texture all its own. The heavy scent of decay filled her nostrils, sweet and cloying as molasses.

Then the dim light returned, and between the close-packed tree trunks there appeared a new pathway, seeming almost like a fairy-tale track leading down what looked like a tree-lined cavern. The branches bent overhead in a leafy canopy—a living tunnel.

Donna turned to Xan, wondering whether she could let go of the twigs and earth now, and was relieved when he dropped it onto the ground. She brushed dirt from her gloves and examined the entrance that had opened. "So, I thought you couldn't do any magic."

He didn't meet her eyes. "Oh, that wasn't really my magic—it was just opening a door to the otherworld. There are plenty of them around. You just have to know where to look."

He turned toward the leafy tunnel. "Let's get this over with."

Donna caught a glimpse of how pale he suddenly looked. How could she blame him? After all he'd lost at the hands of the elves, he was willing to walk back into their territory. For her. She herself was fighting down a feeling of cold dread, trying not to think about the nightmarish creature that had caused her own injuries. The Wood Monster, as it had become known in her dreams. The Skriker.

Xan grabbed her hand again, pulling her forward, and they stepped onto the secret pathway—the Old Path. As Donna placed her foot on the bed of pine needles, it almost felt as though she'd walked through a physical membrane—invisible, but very definitely there. Her ears popped as they pushed their way through and started down the tunnel of arching branches. She became aware of a whispering sound that seemed to come from all around.

Swallowing, Donna ignored the feeling of being watched that was creeping slowly up her spine. She concentrated instead on putting one foot in front of the other. *All*

I need to think about is Navin, she told herself firmly. *That's why I'm here*. Guilt rose inside her, a physical sensation in her chest that made it hard to breathe: they had only taken her friend because of her. Of that she was certain.

Now she just had to find out why.

Fifteen

It was like walking down a shadowy hallway. Donna gripped Xan's hand as tightly as she dared, stepping over dead leaves through the Elflands alongside a half-human guy she'd met only a few days ago. They were in the last remaining home of the wood elves. It felt horribly real.

A clearing opened ahead of them, and Donna knew it would be larger than the previous one. Holding her breath, she felt a blade of sunlight touch her as they passed beneath a gap in the canopy overhead. And then it was gone, and they were plunged once more into near darkness as they headed toward the opening ahead. She found herself walking faster now, just so she could step into the wide open space of the clearing—anything to escape the oppressive feeling of being closed in by trees.

As they emerged from the tunnel, Donna fought to control her breathing and took in the familiar creatures ranged around the clearing. They looked more twisted and grotesque than ever under the shifting shadows of the waving branches. She felt Xan give her hand a squeeze and held on for dear life. She didn't dare look at him.

This clearing was similar to the one in her dream, but there was no tree stump in the center of it. Instead, there was a carved wooden chair, rough-hewn but strangely beautiful, its ragged edges seeming to be part of something living. It was a throne of sorts, draped with ivy and other vines, with white flowers scattered on the ground around it.

Sitting on the throne was a human-shaped figure, seemingly carved out of wood. Donna wondered for a moment if she—for clearly it was a "she"—was wearing an elfskin to change her form in some way, but a deep intuition told her that this was the being's own skin. She seemed more fey, and less twisted and made of earth, than the other wood elves. Donna's legs trembled as she counted six elves standing in a semicircle around the throne, apparently some kind of guard. They half-crouched, muttering, watching her and Xan through slitted black eyes.

"Welcome," said the woman-thing sitting on the throne, in a voice like rustling leaves. "Welcome Donna Underwood, of the iron world."

Then the woman laughed, her nut-brown face creasing into cruel lines and her lipless mouth opening wide. Her mossy hair was long and thick, crowned with brambles and white flowers. There was a belt of long grasses around her slender waist, and Donna's eyes widened as she realized there were hanks of what looked like human hair hanging from it. Elflocks. She swallowed. If the legends were to be believed, these belonged to trapped human souls.

Her breath caught in her throat. *Mom*, she thought, trying to get a better look at the belt.

But the woman-thing was speaking again. "Come here, child. Leave your halfling companion where he is." Her voice hissed with clear disdain.

The sound set Donna's teeth on edge and made her hands and arms throb more than ever. She tried to find the strength to speak. She stepped forward, ignoring Xan's warning tug on her hand. "How do you know my name?"

"We remember you, Donna Underwood. Don't you remember us?" The creature's voice was gentle and deadly at the same time, the strange leafy tones as expressive as the most human of voices.

Donna lifted her chin. "Yes, I remember some of you. But I don't recall *you*…"

"Ah, you were but a young sapling. Please, let us make introductions, as is proper. I am the Wood Queen—ruler of the Elflands, of all that is left of our territory—and these are my kin, the wood elves. I have many names, though some have called me Aliette."

"*Aliette*? Isn't that French?" Donna tried to fit the name to the strange woman before them.

The Wood Queen—Aliette—watched her with expressionless eyes. "That is the closest you will get to my name in your limited language. It serves well enough."

"I wish I could say I was pleased to meet you," Donna muttered. She was terrified, yet there was something so surreal about the whole setting that she could almost believe it was happening to somebody else. Or maybe it was just another dream.

Xan glanced at her, a question on his lips, but he was forced to turn his attention back to the Wood Queen when she spoke directly to him.

"Your name is unknown to us, half-fey creature, but you do not belong here."

"That's not what some of your *kin* thought when they tried to kill me in the Elflands." Xan's voice shook, but not with fear. His barely withheld fury made him seem more powerful and older than he was.

"Did they?" asked the queen, almost nonchalantly. "That may be so, but the past is the past."

Xan stepped forward, his head raised. "How dare you disregard me. I will not be brushed aside so easily, *your majesty*. I demand reparations for what I lost."

Aliette's slitted eyes grew even more narrow. If she'd possessed lips, Donna suspected they would be curled into an expression of scorn right about now. "You are in no position to demand anything, *halfling*."

Although Donna had been trying to follow the conversation, Xan had kind of lost her at "reparations." And she'd been under the impression that his reason for being here was to help her to find Navin. And Maker. She pulled him around to face her, ignoring his resistance while brazenly turning her back on the queen. "What are you *doing*?" she whispered.

Xan was flushed and breathing heavily. "I'm sorry. When I saw her just... sitting there. And those things around her." Xan licked his lips and looked at the ground. "I lost it for a second."

She touched his face—a fleeting gesture that she could only hope transmitted her empathy. "It's okay, Xan."

The queen's voice rang out, making Donna's heart pound suddenly as she spun to face the throne again. "We are wasting time with your trivial nonsense, and I'm sure you don't want to do that—not when there is so much at stake." Her mouth curved up at the corners, a mocking reflection of a human smile. "I'd like to know why you invaded my lands, such as we have left." Aliette shifted on her throne, leaves and vines rustling around her as if blown by an icy wind. She focused her black gaze on Donna. "What do you have to say to me, Donna Underwood of the alchemists? You, whom we now call Iron Witch."

Iron Witch? What was this thing talking about? Donna's eyes widened and she clenched her fists. The name must surely refer to her tattoos, but how would Aliette even know about that? Yet there was no time to reflect on the strange name—almost a title—that the queen had given her. She did her best to stand still, ignoring the wood elves circling the clearing. She and Xan were as good as trapped here—if they ran for it, she didn't know if they could escape. So what did she have to lose by pursuing her reasons for coming in the first place? Donna was grateful for the light pressure of Xan's arm across her back, his warm hand around her shoulder.

She looked directly at the Wood Queen. "I don't know what that means," she said formally. "I just want to know what you've done with my friend, Navin Sharma. And the alchemist, Maker."

There was crackling laughter from the queen, followed by a slow, sly smile. "The boy is safe with us, and will remain so until you bring me what I need."

"And what's that?"

"Why, the secret of eternal life, my dear. What else is there?"

Donna took a step back. "What? Don't you live long enough already? You're practically immortal." She knew what the queen was talking about, but she wasn't about to show it.

"You know that isn't true, girl. We live long, but not as long as we used to. The elves sicken and die, thanks to the spreading disease of the iron world. We will become nothing more than wraiths if I do not find a new way to survive." She fixed Donna with her empty eyes. "All we have ever desired was to live our lives independent of the tithe, free of the rules of our fey cousins."

Donna snorted. "Isn't that what you've achieved?"

The queen's voice was quieter than before. "The price has been...higher than anticipated."

"Be careful what you wish for, your majesty." Donna couldn't help herself. This creature, who held her best friend prisoner, dared to complain about the consequences of the choices she'd made.

Xan stepped forward before Aliette could reply. "We just want to take our people and go. That's all."

Donna felt comprehension dawn, followed quickly by more confusion. "I can see why you'd take Maker as a hostage; he's a powerful enemy and could give you leverage with the alchemists. But Navin...he only means something to me."

"As indeed, Donna Underwood, you mean something to us," replied the queen.

Donna's stomach clenched. She stayed silent and tried to stop her knees from shaking as the queen's words echoed softly in the forest air.

Aliette ran thin brown fingers along the lichen-covered arms of her throne. "There is so much you do not know, daughter of the alchemists. You might do well to ask your archmaster what you were doing in the Ironwood a decade ago."

"What are you talking about?" Donna couldn't stop herself. "Quentin and the Order were rescuing me from your people."

The queen looked... bored, if it were possible for her face to register such an emotion. "And why, exactly, would we steal you from your bed, foolish child? How could we achieve such a thing in the iron world, when you were protected so well?"

Donna's face drained of color; she could feel the flesh of her cheeks stretch tight and her head was suddenly too light. A faint buzzing in her ears made her wonder if she might faint. She didn't understand what this creature was saying.

And then Xan's arm was around her again, supporting her and sharing his warmth. "Don't listen to her, Donna. She's just trying to confuse you."

"Believe what you will," Aliette said. "It is of no consequence to me."

"You're not making sense, your majesty, so how can I believe anything you say?" She was pleased that her voice was steady.

The queen shrugged, dislodging some of the leaves from her shoulders. "What matters is that we have what you want, and you have access to what *we* want. I propose ... a deal. An exchange of resources."

Donna shook her head with a growing sense of panic. "I don't have 'access' to anything!" It was crazy for this creature to think that she—a teenage girl, not yet a full Initiate—would have access to the most precious secret of the alchemists.

The Wood Queen's face contorted into another smile, the cracked bark of her cheeks splitting further. "You will deliver the elixir of life to me. The secret of eternal life abides within those few precious drops hidden among the Order's ranks, and we are dying. Even now the wood elves sicken; I can only provide them with as much power as I have, and the iron world takes its toll even on me." Her face grew sly. "I know the alchemists have it—they are ever working to replicate it. Bring me the vial of elixir and I will let your friend go free."

Donna could taste sharp metal in her mouth and realized that she had bitten her tongue. Her mind raced through what this meant, but it was difficult to think straight while the elves around them whispered and muttered, swayed and circled. A rumor *had* been making the rounds, among the alchemists of all four Orders, that the Order of the Dragon still possessed some of the elixir. Yet even if this was true, Donna had never been entirely convinced about the so-called power of the elixir. She'd seen a lot of strange things in seventeen years, but believing there was something that could convey immortality and heal mortal wounds was quite a stretch. And despite the rumors, she'd never seen any evidence that people like Quentin Frost or Maker were protecting the elixir of life.

But now it seemed that she'd been naïve, and her best friend could be paying the price. The Wood Queen was waiting for her answer. She licked her lips and tried to keep her expression neutral, thinking of the dark elf who'd attacked her and Xan on Ironbridge Common, and the one in Maker's workshop. Not to mention her near certainty that *something* had been watching them when she and Navin left Xan's party. The elves had been following her—tracking her, staking out the places she went to and the people she knew. People she loved, like Navin. And that made them vulnerable. *This* is what happened to people who were crazy enough to care about her.

Donna raised her eyes and gritted her teeth. Enough. That was enough self-pity. She fixed the Wood Queen with a hard stare. "How do I know you'll honor any kind of bargain between us?"

"You don't know, of course. But I will tell you that a deal made in the Elflands is binding. Bound by oak and ash, it is unbreakable as the earth's core."

Donna narrowed her eyes. "I want to see Navin. Bring him to me."

The queen stood, raising herself slowly from the wooden throne and lifting her leafy skirts aside with a low crackling sound so that she could step down from the dais. Her oak-hued skin seemed to shift and fold into new forms as she settled herself a short distance from Donna and Xan, looking down on both of them from her impressive height. She was as tall and straight as a proud tree, unbowed by time and the elements despite her claims that the iron world was weakening her.

As she bent toward Donna, her voice hissed like an angry wind through a forest. "I will show him to you, as a gesture of good faith. But know this, Donna Underwood—you will bring me the elixir or you will never see your friend again."

Gripping her hands into tight fists against the pain in her bones and heart, Donna said nothing. Her whole body seemed to be shaking; no matter how hard she tried, she couldn't stop it. Once again, Xan's arm tightened around her shoulders. He was amazingly calm—or at least he appeared to be on the outside—and she was grateful for that. She could only guess at the pain he must feel, but perhaps his earlier outburst was helping him cope under what must be unimaginably difficult circumstances for him.

The queen whispered a command to a nearby wood elf, and it disappeared through the trees at the far side of the clearing. Donna stepped out of the circle of Xan's arm and looked around, trying to make sense of this place. She cast a sidelong glance at the queen, who was standing statue-still. For a moment it seemed as if she were made out of stone rather than wood.

At the sound of footsteps rustling through the undergrowth, Donna moved forward, reminding herself to keep calm. The thought of seeing Navin again swept all else aside, filling her with hope and trepidation in equal measure. *Please, just let him be all right.* The urge to run toward him was overwhelming.

And then there he was, led between two wood elves and looking all in one piece, apart from a slight limp and a nasty bump on the right side of his head. Even from a distance she could see the dark shadows beneath his eyes, and her heart reached out to him. His arms were tied behind his back with some kind of complicated vine. Hot fury rose in her gut and she tasted the furious urge to smash the creatures holding him.

"Navin!" She couldn't keep herself from calling out. Xan placed a cautionary hand on her shoulder, but she shook him off.

"Donna?" There was uncertainty in Navin's voice, which was not surprising. These creatures were shape-changers and in their natural element here, with far more power than they had in the iron world. Who knows what Navin must be thinking right now?

And then Donna had to face the possibility that this wasn't even the real Navin standing in front of her, his jeans ripped and his hair messy. *No*, she thought. She couldn't let doubt undermine her—she wouldn't allow it. This *was* her friend. It had to be.

"Navin, I'm going to get you out of here." Her voice trembled, but she tried to smile at him.

A ghost of a smile lifted his lips. "Oh yeah, Underwood? You and whose army?" His eyes fell on Xan, and he frowned.

"You remember Xan, right? He's going to help us, Nav."

Navin nodded slowly, looking from Donna to Xan and then back again. His smile seemed sad all of a sudden, the kind you use when you're saying goodbye. "I don't think they're going to let me go, no matter what you do. Maker's here, too. I've only seen him a couple times though."

Donna hated to hear him sounding so resigned, but her heart lifted at the news of Maker. She tried her best to sound reassuring. "Just hang in there. I'll get you home, I promise."

The Wood Queen stepped in front of her, blocking her view. "Now you know he is safe and will remain so, as long as you bring me what we need." She clasped her twiggy fingers in front of her. "Leave our home, now, by the way you entered. Do not bother to return without the elixir. Speak to anyone about this and your friend will die. The old man might not be so lucky." The threat hung in the air, poisonous, suggestive of something worse than death.

Donna swallowed, trying to speak but not sure what there was left to say. She wondered if the queen would know if she went to the Order for help. But no doubt the wood elves would be watching her—they could move like shadows when they wanted to. She knew that already.

Aliette spoke again. "You have until dawn."

Dawn? Panic gripped her and she found it difficult to draw her next breath. It must be mid-afternoon already, which only left her perhaps twelve hours to achieve the impossible.

"That's not enough time." She tried not to sound as pathetic as she felt. She took a step forward, putting more strength into her next words. "I can never get it in time—that's crazy!"

The Wood Queen didn't respond. She simply turned away and headed toward the far side of the clearing. The surrounding wood elves moved forward, clicking and scraping in the backs of their knobbly throats and looking as if they were going to herd Donna and Xan out of the clearing. Donna wondered if any of them could speak, like their queen did. She glanced at Navin, despair welling up within her as he was led away by his guards. He twisted his head around for one last look at her; their eyes met and held.

In that moment, Donna tried to communicate everything she was thinking and feeling. A single glance really *could* say a thousand things, and she hoped she was transmitting even a tiny percentage to her friend.

Xan grabbed her hand and tugged her toward the tunnel. "Come on, Donna, we'd better get out of here."

"I can't leave him. I just *can't.*"

He pulled her closer to him. "You'll be back for him. You promised."

"I did, didn't I?" Donna sniffed, surprised to feel warm tears filling her eyes. "I never break a promise." But even as she said it, she wondered how she could possibly keep this one. Twelve hours to discover the place where the alchemists kept the elixir. What she was facing was impossible and unfair, but that didn't make it any less true.

They walked back along the shadowy path, back through the open door, and out into the tiny clearing. Back through the undergrowth, where there was a sticky moment when Xan wasn't sure if they were headed in the right direction, and finally back onto the main Ironwood pathway.

Donna's hands ached less the farther they got from the faery door, but her heart ached more with each step that took her away from Navin. She turned her mind to the new dilemma: how was she going to find something she wasn't even entirely sure existed? And even if she *did* manage to get it, was she really just going to hand it over to the alchemist's enemies? No, she told herself, don't think about that yet. One step at a time.

She would find a way into Quentin Frost's house and uncover the secrets hidden inside—even if it meant breaking in tonight while he and Simon and the rest of the household were sleeping.

Sixteen

Donna fiddled with the delicate silver charm bracelet around her wrist and tried not to think about her mother. She'd almost left the bracelet, in its little pouch, hidden among her underwear in the bottom drawer of her dresser, but something made her grab it at the last minute. Mom had wanted her to have this bracelet, and maybe it would bring her luck tonight. Xan would be here to pick her up soon, and she would have to get out of the house to meet him without Aunt Paige knowing about it.

She could use all the luck she could get.

Fortunately, Donna had an idea of where to start this impossible search, and it was the best she had to go on. The *only* thing she had to go on. Her "research" had been a simple matter of cross-referencing all mentions of clocks and time with the elixir of life, and she'd been pleasantly surprised at the number of results. She hadn't even needed to Google it; her own school books covered the subject. Apparently, European alchemical recipes often called for the elixir to be stored inside a clock, a symbolic gesture that represented the elixir's legendary ability to slow the effects of time on whomever dared to use it. One particular clock stood out in Donna's mind as she scanned these stories. While she didn't expect things to be quite so easy, at least it gave her a place to start.

Grabbing her coat from the closet, Donna shrugged into its thick warmth, grateful for its length on this cold November night. The dark gray color seemed well suited to covert operations, and she pulled a black wool hat down over her hair for good measure.

She switched off the light and opened her bedroom door a crack, glancing in the direction of Aunt Paige's bedroom. The slit of light under the door meant that her aunt had probably fallen asleep while reading in bed. Relieved, Donna carefully closed her door again.

Then she took a deep breath and did something she hadn't done since she and Navin had first become friends, when they used to visit each other after lights out, their respective guardians thinking they were in bed. She climbed out the window and, using the half-rotten trellis and the drain pipe for support, shimmied down to the ground. The magical strength in her hands and arms always made the task so much easier than it should have been. She only bashed her shin twice, which she took to be a good sign; maybe luck was on her side after all.

The moon was almost full and Donna was glad of the light, but also worried that she might be too easily spotted if anyone happened to be looking out their back windows. Thinking invisible thoughts, she sprinted to the back of the yard, climbed over the fence, and walked down the alleyway that led out onto the main road.

Xan was there waiting, as promised, leaning against his car and holding his cell phone as though expecting her to call. She'd told him that if she had trouble getting out of the house, he would have to create a diversion. Thankfully, that part of the plan hadn't been necessary. His face broke into a grin of pure relief the moment he spotted her.

Donna smiled back and touched his hand. "Thank you for doing this, Xan." She raised herself up on tiptoe and kissed his cheek.

He shrugged, his eyes filled with warmth. "Sure."

She slipped into the passenger seat and buckled up, trying to steady her breathing. This was crazy, she knew, and they were taking a huge risk. She was trying not to think too far ahead, but already it was eleven o'clock and there were only a handful of hours until dawn. Could she really be planning to hand over something so valuable to the alchemists' lifelong enemy? How would she ever explain it to Aunt Paige—or to any other members of the Order? She would be a traitor. And what would her father think of her, if he were alive today? Donna angrily turned her mind away from such thoughts, staring out the window and watching the dark Ironbridge streets pass by.

She would do whatever it took to save Navin. He hadn't asked for this—to become a bargaining piece between warring factions of fey and mortals, themselves fractured remains of an ancient time when things had probably been a hell of a lot simpler. Navin was an innocent bystander, and she wouldn't let him suffer for something that he could never truly understand, no matter how much he might try.

They approached the Frost Estate and parked around the corner, leaving themselves a short walk to the main gate. It would be tricky gaining entry without alerting anyone, Donna knew, especially since there were magical wards in place.

Xan pondered this problem as they huddled by the wall on the south side of the estate. "I think we'll be okay. You're not a threat to them—you come here all the time for classes, anyway—so I doubt you'll trigger any of the defenses."

Donna frowned. "What about you?"

He pushed his hair out of his eyes. "I honestly don't know. If I had the power I should have, I could make myself invisible to most magic. But..."

Donna touched his arm. "It's okay. We'll just have to chance it. Maybe you've got some natural protection that you're not aware of."

"Maybe. And ever since we opened that door into the otherworld I've been feeling different, somehow. As though something is awakening inside me." He shrugged. "I don't know what it means—or if it means anything at all. But it could be a good sign."

He turned and climbed the wall with relative ease. Once again Donna saw how agile he was; was this ability part of his fey heritage? Xan crouched at the top in the darkness, and for a moment all she could see was a shadow cloaked in the familiar black coat. His bright green eyes blinked down at her like a cat's.

And then she was hauled unceremoniously to the top, scrambling slightly as the toes of her sneakers struggled to find purchase against the smooth areas of the wall, until she rolled next to Xan and caught her breath.

Without speaking, they dropped down into the grounds of the Frost Estate.

Donna looked up at Quentin's mansion and bit her lip, wondering what to do next. If only she could've searched for clues during a study break tomorrow ... but there was no time for that. Navin—and Maker—only had until dawn. She glanced over at Xan and wondered what he was thinking.

They were standing outside the window of the Blue Room, but what Donna hadn't accounted for were the wooden shutters closed firmly over it, no doubt locked from the inside. Of course, they could probably break them open, but what sort of noise would that make? And it would be obvious the next day that something had happened.

She caught Xan's eye and raised her eyebrows. "Any ideas?"

"I think we should try the back door."

He shoved his hands into the pockets of his coat and led the way around the house, checking that all the lights were off at the rear as they were in the front. Satisfied that the household had definitely gone to bed (Quentin and Simon weren't young men, and Donna knew they tended to retire close to ten o'clock during the week), they took turns examining the back door.

"I could probably break it," Donna said, "but I don't want to wake everybody up."

Xan crouched down and studied the lock. "This can be picked, I think. I'm sure they have magical wards in place, but those protect against the big threats to security; nobody expects an old-fashioned breaking-and-entering deal. A credit card and something sharp should do it." He pulled his wallet out of an inside coat pocket.

Donna scanned the ground, then searched her pockets for a paperclip or something useful. She wished she were the kind of girl to wear pretty hair clips, because then she could present one to Xan and things would be a whole lot easier. As she dug into her pockets, something sharp pressed against her left wrist, inside her glove. *Wait,* she thought; *maybe there's something here we can use.*

She carefully removed her charm bracelet. There were only six charms on the silver chain, each one soldered in place. Donna's lips curved into a smile—one of the charms was a tiny replica of a dagger. Silently thanking her mother, she pulled off her glove, pinched the silver piece between her forefinger and thumb, and *pulled.*

Glancing regretfully at the twisted link, Donna slipped the bracelet back on and handed the miniature dagger to Xan.

"Perfect," he whispered, and got to work.

She watched as he concentrated on the lock. He stopped once to smile briefly at her before returning his attention to it. Whatever he was doing looked very fiddly to Donna—he was maneuvering the credit card down the side of the door where the catch would be, while twiddling the sharp blade of the tiny silver knife in the lock. He was down there for some time, his long coat pooled like water behind him on the pathway. At one point, Donna was sure she saw him whispering something, his lips moving almost silently as he concentrated.

After a few more minutes—and a few curses and grunts from Xan—there was a muffled *click* and the door sprung open.

"See?" he said triumphantly.

Donna watched him, a suspicious feeling forming in her gut. "How do you know how to do that?"

His face was closed. "You don't know everything about me, Donna Underwood."

"So it seems." But she let it go—for now—as they entered a dark hallway, then took the lead as they made their way to the Blue Room, slipping the bent silver dagger charm into her jeans pocket and making sure to tuck the bracelet back into her glove. Xan had brought a flashlight from the car, but Donna didn't want to chance it while they were moving around. She used her cell phone to cast just enough light to see by as they padded down the hallway.

Creeping around a huge house at night—while the residents slept peacefully on the upper floors—was making Donna increasingly nervous. She was glad for the plush carpeting that helped to keep their steps muffled.

Just as they approached the entrance to the library, a clock began striking midnight. Someone had obviously reset the grandfather clock after Simon had found her trying to figure out how to do it. Donna held her breath as the twelve chimes sounded from beyond the library doors, gritting her teeth until the ringing stopped. She realized that Xan was holding her hand and she hadn't even noticed it; the gentle pressure rubbed the velvet of her glove against her palm. The sensation was both intimate and comforting, standing in the dark with the midnight hour chiming in the background. When the clock finally finished its announcement, Donna tugged her hand free and pushed open the double doors.

As they entered the room, Xan indicated that he was going to switch on the flashlight. She nodded, waiting while he angled the beam around until it rested on the grandfather clock. The surrounding bookshelves looked eerie in the half-light, shadows falling over the piles of books and reminding Donna of her recent nightmare.

Trying to ignore the bleak images that filled her mind, she approached the clock with caution and stood there, just looking at it. Okay, here went nothing. She reached a gloved hand up toward the ivory clock face, shivering as the shadows on the wall moved under the light of Xan's flashlight. She ran her hands over the glass that was covering the timepiece, wondering if she'd missed something before. If Simon hadn't interrupted her, she could have saved a lot of time searching now. Pushing that irritation aside, she focused on the task. There *had* to be an easy way to open this thing.

Could it really be as easy as popping open the casing and finding the elixir inside? Donna couldn't hold back a wry smile. Yeah, she could hope.

Breathing fast, she ran her fingers along the back of the clock, behind the section housing the clock face, searching for some kind of catch. Her fingers hit something small and solid protruding from the wood; with great relief, she flicked the switch and heard a satisfying click near her ear. Stepping back and resting her trembling fingers against the beautifully polished wooden panels on the front, Donna tried to see what she'd accomplished.

For a moment it didn't seem like anything was different, and she cast a confused glance at Xan.

And then she felt cool air brush across her face as the case of the grandfather clock opened. The wooden front swung wide and Donna had to jump out of the way. When she leaned in close again, she could just make out that there was no visible mechanism or catch on the smooth edge of the door.

A thrill ran down her spine. She impatiently gestured to Xan to shine the light inside the clock. Then she screwed up her eyes and tried to see into the complicated inner workings, all cogs and wheels made of polished brass, half hoping it would be easy and she'd find a handy vial of elixir just waiting for her somewhere. Maybe wrapped in black silk like her aunt's Tarot cards, to keep any negative energy from affecting the contents.

There was no vial.

However, there was—at the very bottom of the casement, sitting innocuously on the heavy base underneath the main workings and brass pendulum of the clock—a steel lever with a wooden handle. She reached toward it eagerly.

"Wait," Xan hissed, grabbing her elbow. The flashlight beam swung crazily for a moment. "You don't have any idea what that does."

Biting her lip, Donna met his eyes and tried to look more confident than she felt. "There has to be something here, Xan. Why would there be a secret way of opening the clock if it wasn't hiding something? And look—" Here she gestured at the empty casement, empty of everything but the regular mechanical bits and pieces you'd expect to find inside a grandfather clock. "There's nothing else inside, so this *has* to be what we're looking for. I just know it."

Reluctantly, he released her arm and she turned back to the lever. Heart pounding, sweat trickling down the back of her neck, she gripped the handle tightly and pushed, noticing how easily the mechanism slipped into position. It seemed as though it was used regularly and kept well-oiled.

Then the entire clock sprang silently away from the wall. Just a few inches, but enough to make it obvious that there was a doorway behind it.

"Whoa," said Xan. "Cool."

Donna tried to keep the excitement out of her voice. "Come on," she whispered. "A secret door that Simon's desperate to protect has got to be something good. Let's go."

She pulled the clock farther away from the wall and slipped behind it before Xan could do anything stupid like offer to go first. *No way*, Donna thought. Time was running out, and nothing was going to stop her from discovering a way to save Navin.

The corridor was lined with cold gray stone and tightly packed earth. It became colder the farther away from the entrance they walked. The floor seemed to be tilting slightly, and Donna soon realized that they were heading down into what would be a basement level. Only it wasn't a basement set beneath the *house*—it had to be located beneath the estate grounds, within the property but beyond the outer walls of the mansion.

There was no need for the flashlight or any illumination from a cell phone as they walked, thanks to the strange multicolored gemstones pressed into the tunnel walls at regular intervals. Donna had never seen anything like them, but they provided enough natural light that she and Xan could walk the length of the passageway without falling over one another.

The smell, on the other hand, was disgusting.

It was like rotten eggs combined with bitter vinegar, and Donna had to pull her scarf around her face to keep from gagging. Xan didn't seem quite so affected, although he agreed it was "pretty gross." Donna knew that alchemical experiments often used sulphur, and her anticipation grew at the thought that they might have found Simon Gaunt's laboratory.

Everybody knew where Quentin's lab was—it was no secret that he liked to putter around in there most mornings, and Donna had even caught a glimpse of it through the door once when she was a very small child. The archmaster's study and workshop was on the very top floor of the house, in an attic that had been especially converted so that noise and smells were kept away from the main part of the house. But nobody knew where Simon worked on alchemical matters, or whether he even *had* a lab of his own. This wasn't surprising, since as the official secretary of the Order he wasn't much more than a glorified administrator. Donna had long suspected that Quentin created the job for Simon because of their private relationship.

Around a sharp bend in the tunnel, they suddenly reached the heaviest oak door Donna had ever seen. For a horrible moment she panicked; surely it hadn't all been for nothing. If the door was locked, would her strength be enough to break it down? It was pretty damn solid-looking, and it could also be magically sealed. At least the nasty stench seemed to be fading—either that or she was just getting used to it.

Donna examined the door and breathed a sigh of relief. There didn't even appear to be a lock on it. The only thing visible—apart from the black-painted iron handle—was a strange inscription stamped into a plaque hanging at eye level:

OUR WORK BEGINS
IN DARKNESS AND IN DEATH

"Cheery," Xan noted.

"Yeah, alchemists are a bunch of laughs to hang out with," Donna said with a heavy sigh.

"Actually," he replied, "I'd say spending time with you has given me some of the best moments of my life." His face was totally sincere, but Donna couldn't help the look she gave him. Did he really think that? Flustered, she said the first thing that came into her head. "Yeah, because I'm *so* special."

Xan frowned. "Don't do that."

"Do what?"

"Put yourself down. You shouldn't do that, Donna."

She shrugged, uncomfortable having so much focus put on her. "Well, I can't see how hanging out with me has been too fun. Okay, if you're going to define 'fun' as getting attacked by elves and having to face the worst possible crap that feeds your nightmares, then maybe you'd be right."

His eyes glinted in the near darkness. "You left out the part where the guy gets to kiss the beautiful girl."

Donna was glad the light was so faint at this end of the corridor; she didn't want him to see how much she was blushing. She ignored him and tried the handle, relieved when the knob turned with no resistance.

When they walked into the room beyond, Donna realized that she was finally seeing what a true alchemical laboratory looked like. The room's contents were the stuff of legend—a near perfect match to the depictions in the textbooks she'd studied under Alma's watchful eye. And yet it was so much more. This lab was *real*; there was a feeling of life and work here, a sense that something magical was brewing somewhere in this very room. In comparison, Quentin Frost's pitiful setup paled into insignificance; it seemed like a kid's chemistry set. Which was strange, Donna thought, given that Quentin was supposed to be the leader of the Order—the archmaster.

The evidence before her seemed to indicate that Simon Gaunt was a lot more than just an administrator. Maybe he was a real magus, which was pretty much unheard of among modern alchemical Orders. At last, Donna thought, her suspicions about Simon's behavior over the years had been vindicated. She'd always known there was something shady about the man.

In the center of the large open space ahead of them was a tall, cylindrical brick structure. It was almost as tall as she was, and upon closer inspection Donna saw that it was some sort of a furnace. Xan followed her over to examine the thing. Heat was coming off it in waves, and Donna realized that it was an athanor—an oven which was traditionally kept burning for most of the year.

She gripped Xan's arm, remembering at the last minute to be gentle. "Now I know what the smoke is!" she said excitedly.

Xan eased his arm away. "What smoke?"

"Oh, sorry." Donna shook her head slowly and tried to calm down. "The smoke I see all year round in the far corner of the grounds, beyond the garden. We must be directly underneath that part of the estate."

"So, what is this thing? I mean, it's obviously some kind of furnace, but what does it do?"

Donna grinned. "Let me introduce you to Slow Henry." She swept her arm in a mock-formal arc, as if presenting the athanor to him.

"'Slow Henry'?" Xan's lips were curving into a smile. Her excitement was obviously infectious.

"It's sort of a nickname, because of the steady and reliable service it provides. The athanor burns slowly through all seasons, rarely letting its owner down. Without fire, there'd be no alchemy. Everything starts here."

Who knew alchemy could be interesting? Because this *was* interesting. Maybe if Alma had actually let her see this, she would've paid more attention to her studies

Her eyes were already sweeping the rest of the room. On one wall, a myriad of glass vessels hung from wooden pegs, all different shapes and sizes forming a stunning collection. Donna recognized some of them from her books, but others were completely mysterious. She could see a spirit holder, ran her fingers over an angel tube, and admired a particularly beautiful moon vessel.

At the farthest end of the room, a small shadowed alcove was set back into the stone wall. Donna walked over and saw that it actually opened into another chamber—this one tiny compared to the main room, with only enough space for a slate-gray curtain that fell from the ceiling all the way to the floor. The heavy curtain was attached to a length of rail, which was bent at angles to form a square; it was rather like a giant shower curtain. It reminded her of something a conjuror would have onstage, so that if you stepped inside the space beyond, you might be in danger of disappearing.

Her mouth went suddenly dry as she realized what this was. This was the most sacred area of an alchemist's laboratory, the oratorium—an area for meditation and quiet contemplation. Donna's hand reached out, almost of its own accord, to touch the rough material of the curtain—

"What's this?" Xan called out.

She jumped guiltily, strangely glad of the distraction, and popped her head back into the main chamber to see what he'd found.

Copper tubing zigzagged crazily along the wall. Donna followed it to its source on the floor: a thick, pear-shaped vessel made of an indefinable material. *Simon had a serpent condenser*—that was crazy. An ancient piece of apparatus, the serpent condenser was used to isolate the living essences of any substance. If she remembered correctly, the condenser was an important part of the process used to create *homunculi*—tiny artificial beings infused with the life force of a variety of chemical compounds.

"Xan, this is it!" Donna clapped a hand over her mouth, realizing she'd practically shouted. Not that it really mattered down here, but still … it didn't hurt to be careful.

Xan stared at the condenser as though it might start producing the elixir at any moment. "This thing creates the elixir of life?"

"No, no—I don't mean that." Donna waved her hands, stumbling over her words in her enthusiasm. "This is a serpent condenser. Okay, it's a totally long and boring explanation, but trust me when I say that this is used in a process that supposedly creates miniature life forms. But I don't think it works *without* the elixir."

Xan didn't look impressed. "So?"

"*So?* So why would Simon have a freaking condenser down here if he wasn't actually using it? There'd be no point—it's useless without a drop of the elixir added to a mixture of other compounds. You'd need to do that every time you operated it." Donna never realized how grateful she'd be for the endless hours spent studying historical treatises about alchemical practice.

"This thing's pretty rare, then?" Xan asked, beginning to catch on.

"Right!" she agreed, nodding her head so vigorously that her neck began to ache. "I honestly don't think it would be installed here 'just in case.'"

Which meant that there had to be some of the elixir of life down here. Donna walked to the center of the lab and began scanning everything around them, trying to decide where a magus would hide something so important. How had the Order kept such an incredible secret? Nations fought wars for knowledge and power like this. People had died in the quest for eternal life. Yet here, in an old house on the outskirts of Ironbridge, she was on the verge of uncovering possibly the greatest discovery of all time.

Her brain hurt just thinking about it.

Then she noticed a workbench in a shadowed corner, covered with a variety of interesting-looking objects. She practically ran over to it and started sifting through pieces of metal, gold coins, containers of herbs and mineral compounds, and all kinds of other mystical paraphernalia.

"Don't just stand there," she said, frowning over her shoulder. "Help me look."

Xan wandered over and started searching at the opposite end. "So what exactly are we looking for?"

"A glass vial of liquid."

He stopped sorting and raised an eyebrow, leaning his hip against the bench. "And what color is this liquid supposed to be?"

Donna bit her lip. *Oh please, memory*, she implored, *don't fail me now.* "Um...red?"

"You don't sound too sure of that."

"It's red." She nodded once, for emphasis.

"Okay, good."

"red...ish."

Xan rolled his eyes and went back to work.

There were shelves above the bench—shelves piled with yet more intriguing artifacts, as well as files and folders filled with paperwork. Considering that Simon was in charge of organizing all of the Order's business, he certainly wasn't very tidy down here, Donna thought.

She reached up on tiptoe, her fingers coming into contact with something solid on one of the higher shelves. It reminded her of a smooth rock—maybe some kind of carving. She extended her arm as far as she could, stretching tall in order to grab whatever was tucked away. The cool outer shell of the object felt like it might be marble; or perhaps some kind of metal? As her hand closed around a heavy base and she carefully lifted the object down, Donna heard an ominous *click*.

The bronze statue in her hand started to scream.

Seventeen

D onna shrieked and dropped it.

It fell to the stone floor with a heavy thud, but the bronze carving of a man's head continued to scream. Its lips were twisted into a grotesque expression of pain, its mouth wide open and an honest-to-god actual *human scream* coming from it.

"Shut it up!" Xan yelled, his green eyes wide and desperate.

"I don't know how!" Donna stared in horror at the thing as it rocked back and forth on the ground. The blank eyes and hooked nose gave it a kind of gargoyle-like appearance, but it was definitely supposed to look like a man. A man with curly hair—also molded from bronze—and a thin mouth that was still screaming.

Xan pushed her out of the way and lifted his heavily-booted foot.

"No, wait," Donna cried, trying to grab hold of his coat and pull him back.

But either he couldn't hear her over the noise or he chose not to hear her, because the next moment Xan had stamped down on the screeching face.

"*Ungh!*" said the statue, then fell silent.

For a moment, the only sound in the lab was the quiet rumbling of Slow Henry. Donna took a shuddering breath and looked at the bronze head, which was now just an inanimate statue—an old-fashioned bust molded to portray a guy who might once have been an alchemist. Its eyes seemed dead and hollow, and there was something undeniably...*evil* about the thing.

Screaming statues were a whole new level of crazy. As far as Donna's knowledge of alchemy went, this was something unheard of—it was a kind of magic that made her flesh crawl and all the hairs on the back of her neck stand up. It was clearly a warning system; she'd triggered some sort of magical alarm by lifting the bronze head from the shelves. What was Simon Gaunt *doing* down here? This wasn't just a regular prop in alchemical transformative work, she'd bet her life on it.

Rubbing her hand across her mouth, Donna continued to stare at the silent lump of carved metal. "What do you think we should do with it?"

Xan looked as grossed out as she was. "I have no idea. This is *your* area of expertise, not mine."

She shivered. "I don't know anything about *this*."

"Maybe we should put it back where you found it—"

The words had only just left his mouth when the sound of muffled footsteps from beyond the door reached them.

"Crap!" Donna took a deep breath to steel herself and grabbed the head off the floor, practically flinging it back into position and scanning the laboratory for a decent hiding place. If someone found them in here, they were so dead. Donna would be hauled in front of Quentin, and her aunt would be horrified and disappointed—not to mention what they'd make of a half-fey guy learning about alchemical secrets. She tried not to imagine what Simon's reaction would be; invading an alchemist's private space and touching his magical tools would have been considered a major offence in earlier centuries. The penalties for such crimes were severe.

Her eyes focused on the alcove that housed the oratorium. It was bad enough just being inside the lab, so what she was considering doing now was the worst kind of sacrilege—but what choice did they have?

The footsteps came closer and then stopped.

"In here," Donna hissed, pushing Xan toward the small chamber.

There was no time for second thoughts. They ducked inside the curtain, Donna arranging the heavy folds behind them as carefully as her shaking hands would allow.

"What is this place?" Xan whispered.

"Oratorium. That must be Simon's altar." Donna nodded at the solid wooden table, the only thing in the cramped space apart from themselves. She tried to swallow the guilt that made her stomach hurt.

The laboratory door opened, then banged shut. Donna jumped, grabbing onto Xan's coat as though she could maybe hide inside it. She realized that his arms had closed around her, and despite the fear of discovery it felt so good ... safe and warm, even though she hated to admit it because it made her feel like she *needed* that safety. She didn't want to be that pathetic girl always running to the guy for help. But sometimes, she was slowly beginning to learn, it was okay to admit you needed help and support. And it was nice to feel she could lean on someone other than Navin for a change.

As that thought struck her, and a picture of an exhausted Navin filled her already anxious mind, Donna backed away from Xan and looked around. Whoever was in the main room was muttering under his breath and moving things around on the workbenches. She couldn't be sure whether it was Simon or not, but it was a pretty good bet. Had he come running after hearing the screaming statue? But surely he'd been too far away... Perhaps the Order's secretary couldn't sleep and was just doing some late-night work.

"We need to get out of here," hissed Xan.

Way to state the obvious, Donna thought. She ignored him and began checking out the sacred objects on the altar. Apart from some medallions with alchemical symbols for various compounds and a container of what looked like salt, the main feature on the altar was a copper-clad box the size of her mother's jewelry box.

But she knew it wasn't a jewelry box. Catching her breath as she reached toward it, Donna wondered if she dared to look inside. This was an incubator, a container traditionally used to hold the *prima materia*—the first matter. Weird to think that Alma had been droning on about this just this week during one of their lessons. Was it only yesterday? She frowned as she tried to remember. It might as well have been last year.

If the incubator really did hold some of the *prima materia*, then she was in big trouble. Nobody but the alchemist who found it could touch it or even *look* at it. Which always seemed a bit silly to Donna. After all, you couldn't create first matter; as one of the building blocks of reality it just... *existed*. So how could it really belong to any one person?

Oh well, she thought. Too late for regrets.

The box was entirely sealed, with no visible way of opening it, but Donna knew that underneath the copper it was made of roughly hewn wood, the more natural the better. She wouldn't be surprised if it was fashioned out of cuttings from the Ironwood. Pausing to listen to what was happening in the other room, she heard the sounds of clinking glass and a louder thrum from the furnace—Slow Henry's door must have been opened.

She picked up the incubator and wondered what on earth Simon Gaunt was doing, keeping a tiny piece of the universe in his lab.

As Xan watched, Donna crushed the box between her gloved hands as though balling up a piece of paper. The wood beneath the copper coating split with a sharp crack, making her heart beat so loudly she thought for sure it would be heard, even above the sound of coal being heaped into the furnace.

She held her breath for a moment, staring into Xan's green eyes, but nothing happened. Then she began to pull the broken pieces of the incubator's lid away from the cracked base.

Donna wasn't surprised to see the handful of black earth that spilled onto the altar. What made her eyes almost bug out of her head was the shining glass vial, half buried in the dark and earthy substance.

Heart in her mouth, she carefully extracted it from the half-ruined box.

The vial was all in one piece. It was the length and width of her little finger, and held what could barely be two or three drops of blood-red liquid, right at the very end.

Xan met her eyes and they both breathed a sigh of relief. He shook his head, a nervous smile playing on his lips. "That was close," he whispered. "You could've broken it."

Donna felt sick. She had almost destroyed her one chance of saving Navin.

But she *hadn't*, and now she held something that could supposedly create new life, heal all kinds of illness, and even bestow immortality. She gazed at the warm ruby glow as she swirled those precious few drops around the vial.

The elixir of freaking life, right here in Simon's lab. Maybe the earth in the incubator wasn't even the real deal; there was every chance it was just regular dirt from the gardens, used to hide the true contents of the box. Sucking in a breath, Donna dug in her pocket and pulled out the little pouch that her mother's charm bracelet had been in. She dropped the vial inside it and pushed the tiny package as deeply into her coat pocket as she could.

She couldn't quite believe she'd done it. But getting her hands on the prize was one thing; now, they had to get it out of here in one piece. Navin and Maker's safety depended on her delivering the elixir to the wood elves.

But could she really give up something so valuable?

She heard the door to the athanor slam shut with a clang that echoed all the way into their small room. Simon must have finished restocking Slow Henry. Donna nudged Xan and pulled his head down so she could whisper in his ear. "Maybe that's all he was doing."

Their faces were almost touching.

Xan nodded. "Right. I guess someone has to keep it going, especially if it runs for most of the year."

Footsteps slowly moved away. Donna guessed they were heading toward the door. *Oh, please*, she prayed, *please let him be leaving*.

The heavy door banged shut.

"Now!" Donna whisper-shouted. "We have to get out of here."

"Wait, let him get farther along the corridor," Xan said, frowning and trying to resist as she tugged him toward the curtain she was already lifting aside.

"I don't want to stay trapped in here," she replied. "Come on, Xan, *please*. We have to leave!"

They ran back into the main chamber. Donna licked her lips and scanned the area. Grabbing Xan's hand, she dashed across the length of the laboratory, gritting her teeth as they passed the shelf holding the statue.

The bronze head woke up.

It seemed to have recovered from being stomped on, and began screaming and yelling as though someone was trying to melt it for scrap. *Which sounds like a pretty good idea*, Donna thought savagely.

Footsteps clattered back toward the lab.

Xan made as if to go back into the oratorium.

She shook her head. "No, he'll look in there!"

Xan frowned for a moment, then nodded toward the floor. Donna could see where Xan thought they should hide, but she wasn't entirely convinced it would work.

But as the handle on the door turned, she decided it was the best plan they had.

They dove beneath the workbench, cramming themselves into the space between the legs. It was a tight squeeze, but they made it just as the door opened and someone strode into the chamber.

The bronze statue continued to yell—directly above them.

Donna wondered if the thing could actually see. Is that how it worked? Or did it simply make that awful noise whenever somebody disturbed it; somebody particularly dumb like *her*. She grimaced at the racket and tried not to think about the fact that she was half-sitting on Xan's lap. There wasn't space to move—hardly room to *breathe*. She wondered how he was handling it, considering how much taller he was.

Xan's arms went around her and he pulled her hard against him. Donna had been trying to keep a *few* of her body parts from being plastered against his, but it was pretty much impossible and her legs ached from the effort. At least now she could relax against him and it didn't feel as though every muscle in her body was going to explode. He was so *warm* ... she'd noticed that about him before, like on the night that he'd kissed her.

As soon as *that* thought entered her head, she couldn't help looking up into his face. Their noses almost touched. Donna could just about make out the laughter lines crinkled around his eyes in the half light. He must be smiling, but she was too close to be able to see his mouth. How could he be smiling at a time like this? The boy definitely had a reckless streak, and she couldn't help being drawn to it. She'd always been so careful in her life, and now here was somebody who took risks and flirted with her when they were seconds from potential discovery.

It was totally sexy.

From where they were crouched, they could see a pair of legs approaching the bench. Donna held her breath and imagined that she was invisible. The legs were clad in burgundy pajamas that were a little too short, revealing thin white ankles and veiny feet squeezed into brown slippers. *Yuck*. Definitely Simon.

"Be silent," the alchemist said, his voice cold.

Donna jumped, and it was only Xan's quick reflexes that stopped her from bumping her head on the underside of the workbench. She concentrated on slowing down her breathing.

She also prayed that the statue alarm system couldn't rat them out.

Miraculously, the bronze head seemed to respond to Simon's command. Blissful silence reigned in the laboratory.

His feet moved as he reached upwards. "Has somebody else been in here?"

Donna was sure she could taste her own fear as her heart beat faster. Or was it Xan's heartbeat she could feel? Pressed against each other as they were, she could hardly tell where she ended and he began. Her legs were tangled up with his and her cheek was resting on his shoulder. His hand held the back of her neck in a gentle grip, his thumb moving nervously beneath her ear.

The bronze statue spoke, almost reluctantly, as though the words were being dragged from it. Its voice was high-pitched and sounded far away. "Two people, master. The oratorium."

Relief flooded into Donna's limbs. She slumped, her nose pressed into Xan's neck, and took a shuddering breath.

She pulled herself together as Simon's feet retreated toward the alcove.

"Ready?" she mouthed, fixing Xan with a determined stare.

He nodded, and they burst from beneath the workbench and dashed across the chamber, through the open doorway, and out into the corridor.

Eighteen

Donna ran until she thought her chest would burst. Her lungs burned and her legs felt like two heavy stones, but she kept pumping her arms and didn't look back until they were all the way to other end of the passageway.

Xan led the way as they bolted through the narrow opening behind the grandfather clock, then slammed it shut behind them. Donna cringed as she heard the ancient gears and mechanical workings rattle inside the casing.

"Oops," he said.

She glared at him. "You're going to wake the rest of the household up."

"Well, as long as there's not another secret exit from the *secret lab*"—he waggled his eyebrows—"that dude in slippers can't get out."

Donna resisted the temptation to roll her eyes. "Like he won't know how to operate the mechanism from the inside. It's *his* secret lab."

Xan shrugged. "We'd better get out of here—we've got what we came for."

Nodding, Donna ran her hand over the small bulge in her coat pocket. She just needed to make sure it was there. *The elixir!* She could hardly believe it, even now. She checked that the clock's case really was properly shut, and then gazed at the ivory face once more. "Damn," she hissed. "Look, it's stopped."

Xan was next to her in a flash. "Yeah, and look at the time. Just after midnight—the exact time we opened it."

"We can't worry about that now." Using her cell phone as a guiding light once more, Donna ran over to the doorway of the library and checked the silent corridor for signs of movement.

She was about to step out into it when she heard a sharp *click* from somewhere above them.

She froze, her heart going like a piston. She couldn't help wondering, if she ever survived this night, how many years she'd taken off her potential lifespan.

Xan laid a hand on her shoulder. "Sounded like a door closing."

"What?" Donna demanded, trying to keep her voice down despite her rising panic.

"There's someone coming down the stairs."

Donna strained to listen. "Are you sure?"

"Absolutely. There's someone moving around up there—sounded like they went *up* some stairs and now they're coming back down again."

"Maybe they're just coming down to the kitchen…"

His mouth was set in a grim line. "Or maybe they're coming this way."

Donna moved to a window and pushed it open as far as it would go. "Over here, quickly."

"What are you doing?" hissed Xan.

"We have to get out of here. *Now*."

Glancing once more at the door, he joined her at the window and began to unlatch the shutters, swinging them back against the outside wall of the house.

"You first," she said.

"Don't be stupid—"

Donna pushed him. Hard. "No time to argue. You. First." She enunciated each word and glared at him. There was no way she would let someone she cared about get hurt because of her—not ever again.

Then the sound of banging started, from behind the grandfather clock.

Xan cursed and swung his legs over the thick stone ledge. Even though they were on the ground floor, it was still pretty high up. The window overlooked a dip in the garden—which looked weirdly like a moat, though Donna had never thought of it that way before.

She caught Xan's eye once more before he could disappear. She had a bad feeling in her stomach—as though something bad was going to happen, but she couldn't quite put her finger on what. Xan touched her cheek and gave her a quick smile. And then he was gone, turning around and half-climbing, half-sliding down the grassy embankment. He landed with an audible thump, making her wince.

Climbing up onto the windowsill, Donna edged forward, gasping in shock as the cold air hit her face. She crab-walked a couple of steps until she had one foot outside the window, resting on the stone ledge, and the other still inside the room.

At that moment, as Donna glanced down and saw Xan waiting for her to jump, the Blue Room's light snapped on. She swung round to find herself facing Quentin Frost, standing in the doorway in pajamas and a navy blue dressing gown. She quickly whipped her head back around so that he would only be able to see her hair, covered in the black woolen hat.

"Hey there!" Quentin shouted. "Stop!"

A final thump from the other side of the clock punctuated the archmaster's words, and Donna risked a glance over her shoulder to see Simon throwing himself out of the narrow gap.

She didn't hesitate; gathering her coat around her so that it wouldn't snag on anything, she let herself drop away from the ledge. There wasn't time to feel scared—Donna just trusted that Xan would catch her as she dropped like a stone toward him, her stomach rising up as she fell down. Air whistled past her face and her arms spread wide, as though she might be able to fly.

She landed with a clash of bones, although Xan actually did manage to catch her before they tumbled in a heap on the ground. Donna sprawled across his torso and felt a guilty rush of adrenaline as she realized his arms were enclosing her body; she could hear him breathing heavily in her left ear.

They disentangled themselves, and Donna shivered when his hand brushed her ribs as he helped her clamber to her feet. She spared a glance back at the window.

Simon Gaunt stood silhouetted against the light, his right hand raised as though about to throw something. Donna grabbed Xan's arm and tugged desperately. "Run!"

They ran full-pelt toward the estate's wall. Donna veered off to the right, heading for a small clump of trees, but Xan seemed to be taking a more direct route. Her breathing was labored and her heart slammed against her chest as she glanced back; lights were coming on all over the mansion, illuminating the windows and casting shards of brightness onto the well-tended lawn.

Putting on a final burst of speed, Donna reached the wall after what felt like an eternity, gasping for breath and bent double as she tried to compose herself. Xan was waiting for her—he hardly seeming winded at all, damn him—and she had a good view past the trees, back to the house. She could just make out two people searching the grounds—Simon must have started rousing the staff. There weren't many searchers, but enough to make it urgent that they get the hell out of there as quickly as possible. Knowing Simon Gaunt, he'd probably called the police already, Donna thought bitterly. Simon was so efficient and proper about administrative things, although a little voice told her that perhaps this time would be different. He would have found the broken incubator in his meditation space.

He would know that the elixir was gone.

Xan helped her up and over the wall, and it was just a short sprint to the car. It looked like they had made it, but Donna wouldn't feel safe until they'd put a healthy distance between themselves and the Frost Estate.

As they pulled away and drove through the gates—Xan checking in the rear-view mirror for signs of anyone following—Donna felt a gut-wrenching twist of dismay. She peeled off her woolen hat and undid her coat, wondering what on earth was the matter with her. They were getting away, weren't they?

And then she knew. The sickening realization crept up on her like a bad case of food poisoning. She ran her hands up and down her arms and double-checked the sleeves of her coat, just in case.

"Shit," she said quietly. "My charm bracelet is missing."

She'd gone over the possibilities a hundred times, but she knew she must have lost her bracelet somewhere in Quentin's house. Worse than that, it most likely had fallen off in Simon's lab. And here she'd thought it would bring her luck. Donna put her head in her hands and moaned softly

"Maybe it fell off in the grounds somewhere; that wouldn't be so bad," Xan offered.

Donna breathed out a heavy sigh. "How exactly would that 'not be so bad'? Don't you think that Quentin—or Simon, at least—will have every inch of the grounds searched?"

Xan glanced briefly toward her, then fixed his gaze back on the windshield as he guided the car around a bend in the road. "I thought you said the bracelet was new. Maybe they won't connect it to you."

Donna shook her head and shot him a guilty look. "It's not that simple. Yeah, the charm bracelet is new to *me*, but it was my mother's. She gave it to me when I visited her this weekend. Even if Simon doesn't know it belonged to her, my aunt certainly will."

She pressed the window control and waited impatiently for the glass to slide all the way down. Fresh air always helped when her mind was clogged up like an old vacuum cleaner; she used to take long walks whenever she needed to clear her head. Losing both parents (and not understanding what was wrong with her mother), along with the problems she'd faced at school, had made her feel separate from the world. Walking had helped her feel connected again—to her physical environment if nothing else. She wished she could get out of the car right now and walk all the way to the Ironwood.

Donna put a hand in her coat pocket and felt the reassuring shape of the vial. Pulling it out into the open, she tested its weight as though weighing its value. How much was she willing to give up—what was she *really* willing to sacrifice for Navin?

She closed her eyes, feeling the chill breeze ruffling her hair, then squeezed her eyes tight before opening them again. She cleared her throat. "I can't believe the Order had some of the elixir all this time," she said in a low voice. "I've always suspected they were working toward creating more of it, because there's so little remaining—or none at all. But the elixir of life has a crazy number of ingredients, and there are up to *fifteen steps* you have to follow to create it. The philosopher's stone is needed for the final stage of the process; it's like the match that lights the fuse."

And of course, she thought, the philosopher's stone has been missing for centuries. Its last known location? London, England.

Xan looked like he was about to say something, but then squinted out the window as something ran into the bushes at the side of the road. *Just a cat, or maybe a raccoon*, Donna thought as her heart began to pound. Every shadow seemed full of potential danger. She tried to remember to breathe.

"Maybe the vial really is all they have left," Xan said.

Which she'd already wondered about, of course—and it didn't make her feel any less guilty about even *considering* turning it over to the enemy.

She took in one last lungful of freezing air before closing the window. It felt like her head might burst; the pain that had been building at the base of her skull was slowly spreading. She turned to watch Xan as he pointed the car in the direction of the Ironwood.

"So, what are we really going to do with the elixir?" he suddenly asked. "We can't just hand it over to Her Royal Badness like good little children."

Donna ran her hands through tangled hair, pushing stray strands off her cold face. "Honestly? I have no idea. As much as I want to save Navin—and believe me, I *will* save him one way or another—the more I think about it, the more it scares me to even imagine handing this over. Who knows what they really want it for?"

"Well, if we're being totally honest here, I gotta say I'm not too sure who the real bad guys *are*." Xan looked over at her. "Don't take this the wrong way, Donna, but from what I've seen so far, your Order of the Dragon seems pretty damn shady."

For a moment she couldn't bring herself to reply. The thing was...Xan was right. Over the past week—and even before that—she'd felt her faith in the "rightness" of the Order begin to erode. Of course, she now knew that the real Maker was not, in fact, doing experiments on wood elves in his workshop, but this knowledge hadn't restored her faith. All it did was add to her confusion.

"I know," she said finally. "What we just saw in Simon's lab..." Her voice trailed off and she blew out a frustrated sigh. "I've never seen anything like that before."

"You mean, the possessed statue? Yeah, that was *nasty*."

"Do you think it *was* possessed?" Donna shivered. "It did feel...sort of wrong, somehow. Twisted and dark."

"Whatever it was, we were lucky it couldn't see us under that bench. I thought we were caught for sure."

That was one sentiment that Donna could get behind. As to the rest of it, she just wasn't sure. And each minute that now passed brought them closer to the Wood Queen and the waiting elves; closer to the possibility that she could save Navin.

And she still didn't know what the hell she was going to do.

Nineteen

The dark green leaves and ragged branches of the Ironwood waited, silent, under a full moon bruised by
indigo clouds. Donna shivered, even in her warm coat and
hat. She wished Xan would put his arm around her, then
immediately berated herself for thinking like that when
Navin was in such danger. What was wrong with her? She
sighed, and was surprised to find that she was still shaking
after their escape from the Frost Estate.

They were tramping through the undergrowth, in
search of the entrance to the Old Path they'd used before.

Donna had been quiet ever since they'd entered the Iron-wood again; she couldn't stop thinking about what was ahead of them, and all that had happened to her since meeting Xan at the party just this past Saturday. Her hand closed reflexively on the small pouch in her pocket, as though seeking reassurance that it was still there. Some-how, just knowing that the vial was safely in her possession gave her the strength to continue.

Xan came to an abrupt stop, his eyes wide.

The sound he'd heard made Donna's blood freeze. Distant, otherworldly screams echoed through the trees, making her ears hurt and setting her teeth on edge. Her heart felt as though it had stopped beating, and her whole body was suddenly overcome with weakness. She felt as if she was about to faint.

It was like a high-pitched screeching, scraping along her nerves like fingernails on a chalkboard. It sounded like a small child being murdered.

If she didn't know any differently, she might have thought it was the sound of foxes. How she wished it was just foxes.

Xan met her gaze and she knew he saw her fear—his own face registered something she couldn't identify. His eyes were guarded, their usual glow faded to a deep moss color, but there was something in his expression that let her know he wasn't as cool as he might like her to think. "What was that?"

Donna swallowed, unable to get past the dryness in her throat. "*That* was our cue to move as fast as possible."

He stopped her from walking past him, his hand gripping her arm above the elbow. "Was it what I *think* it was?"

She knew she was being horribly defensive, but she couldn't help it. "I don't know what you're thinking, Xan. I'm not a mind reader."

Undeterred, Xan trailed his hand down her arm until he could clasp her fingers gently in his. "The Skriker."

He made it a statement, so she didn't bother to reply, although she didn't take her hand out of his when they continued walking.

Xan led the way off the main path and they battled through the crowded bushes and ferns she recognized from their earlier trip, Xan once again pushing the brambles aside so she could climb through.

They arrived in the tiny clearing and stood close together. The trees seemed to loom over them, casting shadows upon shadows in the moonlight. Donna shivered, feeling that same heaviness resting on her shoulders and pushing at the base of her skull. She tried to make her breathing shallow as she anticipated the rotten smell of the damp, mossy tree trunks, but it was impossible to avoid smelling it. She wrinkled her nose.

Xan repeated the ritual magic that would allow them to walk the Old Path, gathering dirt and leaves from the cold earth. Donna knew that when he raised his head his eyes would once more be brightest viridian. The closer to the heart of the Ironwood they got, the more fey he became. The thought both scared and excited her.

He stood before her, his hands full of earth and twigs. "Hold on to this like last time, Donna."

They were linked by nature and magic as Xan spoke the ancient words that would open the door and take them into the Elflands. His skin glowed golden, seeming to compete with the cool moonlight that surrounded them, and his eyes sparkled brightly. Donna caught her breath as she felt the tug of power in her stomach and waited for her hands to start hurting.

The sudden wave of darkness wrapped itself around them, momentarily blocking out the dim light, and the scent of damp decay rose up. The smell almost made her gag as it crept between her lips and down her throat.

Then the choking blackness unfolded itself from them; Donna was relieved to once again see a fleeting glint of moonlight through the tall trees. And there was the Old Path, with trees lined up along either side and the green canopy overhead that made it feel more like a tunnel. Dry leaves and branches rustled and cracked underfoot as she took the lead, despite Xan's protests. They walked down it, toward the clearing where she knew Navin was waiting. The thought of confronting the dark elves made her stomach tighten and her heart beat faster, but she tried to calm her breathing and think only of her best friend. He needed her.

The leafy roof finally opened out, and they stepped into the large clearing. Donna caught her breath as the sky appeared above her once more. It looked different, somehow, as though something in the world had shifted and they were on another continent. It was still nighttime, and the moon peeked out from behind the clouds with stars scattered haphazardly around it, but everything looked closer to the ground—as though she could easily reach out and touch that velvet sky.

The clearing was empty, the ivy-draped throne standing in the center as though it hadn't been occupied for years. Moss crept up its wooden sides and into the seat, and Donna wondered if it was possible for time to move at a different rate here. There was an ageless, untouched quality to the air, as though it hadn't been breathed for centuries and Donna and Xan were disturbing it just by their presence.

She turned slowly in a circle, foreboding making her stomach cramp and her throat dry. "This is weird. I expected it to be the same as earlier. I thought she was waiting for us."

Xan nodded. "And she would know the minute somebody breached the door between our world and the Elflands."

Donna walked toward the throne, frustration building within her. Was Aliette playing games with them? Had she lied? "We don't even know where they're keeping Navin, so what should we do?"

And then a shaft of moonlight fell onto the far side of the clearing as the Wood Queen entered, flanked by her six guards. They simply materialized among the trees and walked slowly forward, the pale glow of the moon making their gray-brown skin look sickly and old. They seemed less substantial than before, somehow. Weaker. Perhaps the queen hadn't been exaggerating about their decline.

Then Donna cried out, recognizing Navin being prodded out from beneath the trees by one of the wood elves. His hands were bound behind his back and he looked tired and worn, but he was *there*. She desperately wanted to go to him, but knew that it was pointless to even try. *Not yet*, she thought. *Be patient.*

His dark eyes lit up at the sight of her. Donna tried to smile reassuringly, but she could only manage a half-hearted effort—her throat seemed suddenly too tight and she had difficulty swallowing past the lump there.

"Donna, you shouldn't have come back here," Navin called, his voice surprisingly strong.

She shook her head. "Don't be ridiculous. I would *never* leave you!"

His familiar lopsided grin flashed. "Yeah right, Underwood. That's what you told me Saturday night before leaving me high and dry with the Geek Squad."

Donna burst out laughing; she couldn't stop herself. The relief that he was actually cracking jokes—even bad ones—was just so wonderful.

The Wood Queen swept onto her throne and settled herself regally, waiting for her minions to gather more closely around her. Two elves pushed Navin forward until he stood to one side of her carved wooden seat. The creature who seemed to be in charge of the prisoner planted twiglike fingers on Navin's shoulders and pushed him to his knees.

"Have you brought it?" The queen's brown face seemed more lined than before, and her black eyes were dull and sunken. There was something undeniably *tired* about Aliette. Donna suddenly realized that since the elves had been walking easily in the iron world, holding elaborate glamours in place, they must get their power from her. The Wood Queen was the main source of energy for her kin—but where did she get *her* power?

"I have it, your majesty." Donna's voice rang out clearly. She thought of her mother and tried to catch a glimpse of the locks of hair hanging from Aliette's belt, but the shadows made it difficult to see.

The queen leaned forward, unable to contain her eagerness. "Then give it to me, girl, and you can take the boy and leave."

Xan glanced anxiously at Donna and she flashed him a reassuring look; she knew how much he wanted to secure Maker's freedom, too.

"We won't leave without both Navin *and* Maker," she said. Her voice was steady. Once again, Xan's hand rested in the small of her back, giving her comfort.

"I don't believe that was the arrangement," grated the Wood Queen. The surrounding elves made loud clicking sounds in their throats and seemed to crouch lower, their black eyes staring at Donna with unnerving malice.

"You didn't honestly think I'd leave Maker here, did you?" Donna asked, swallowing her dread. "Either we leave safely with both of them, or you won't be getting anything from me."

Aliette sneered, her cracked face looking more than ever like the bark of an old tree. "And what—foolish child—is to stop me from *taking* the elixir from you?"

"Because I happen to know that what I've found is all that remains. The final drops of the elixir of life. If you force me to do it, I'll make sure you never get your hands on it."

The queen's eyes narrowed to ebony slits, her lipless mouth opening in an ugly gash of rage. "How dare you threaten me!"

Her voice scraped along Donna's nerves and made her stomach clench; the ache in her hands increased, but she refused to show any sign of fear.

Stepping forward, she shook off Xan's restraining hand. "Either you let us all leave safely, or I'll destroy it." She desperately hoped her face held absolute conviction, and that the queen couldn't hear the frantic beating of her heart.

The trees whispered and shook their leaves as the Wood Queen rose from her throne. She grabbed Navin by his thick black hair and wrenched back his head. She was holding a dagger carved out of some sort of dark wood; it looked smooth and sharp, its handle elegantly shaped in a curve that wrapped around her gnarled fingers.

Donna gasped and tried to run forward, but her way was immediately barred by two crouching, hissing wood elves. She felt Xan's arms wrap around her waist and pull her back, her feet dragging in the cold earth as she tried to resist. "Let me go!" she yelled.

Xan's grip was firm and he shook her, whispering fiercely in her ear. "Stop it, Donna. She won't do anything while we've got the elixir." His mouth was virtually touching her earlobe, his cheek brushing against strands of her hair.

She wrenched herself from his arms, gasping, then stood still as a stone, gazing in horrified fascination as Aliette stroked the strange blade along Navin's exposed throat, his vulnerable flesh stretched taut across his Adam's apple.

"Well, well." The Wood Queen's expression might have been a smile, if she'd possessed a human face. "Perhaps you can be persuaded to be reasonable after all, Donna Underwood."

Navin was breathing heavily, but his dark eyes met Donna's without fear. "Whatever they want, don't do it. Not for me," he murmured.

Donna ignored him and tried to get her expression under control. "If you harm my friend in any way, you will *never* get what you want."

"It appears we're at an impasse," replied the queen, in her voice of dead leaves. "How unfortunate."

"It's only unfortunate if you hurt any of my friends."

Xan nodded, joining her. "Including Maker."

"Right," Donna said. "We don't even know if he's safe."

The Wood Queen sneered, but gestured to the creature closest to her. She whispered something in their strange language of clicks and scraping sounds, and the elf ran back into the trees.

Moments later, Donna's eyes lit up as she saw Maker being pushed forward. The old alchemist seemed unharmed on the surface; he walked with a pronounced limp, but that was normal for him, and he looked grubby and tired, with bits of leaf and twig stuck to his gray hair and beard, but other than that he looked remarkably healthy. Donna almost smiled—Maker was a fighter, there was no doubt in her mind about that, as he had proven time and time again when they'd argued over her treatment and rehabilitation.

"Maker!" she called.

The old man's eyes fell on her and widened in shock. "Donna! What are you doing here, child?"

She almost rolled her eyes at being called "child" by yet another person, but she was too pleased to see him to really care. "At the risk of sounding like a clichéd movie, I'm here to rescue you."

Maker didn't get the reference, but she could see the battle between concern and relief playing out on his exhausted face.

The queen swept her hand wide. "See? Here is your Maker. Unharmed, despite what he would do to my kin."

Donna tried not to show any reaction, biting her lip. What did Aliette mean? But before she could think about it any further, the Wood Queen rose to her full height and looked down on the small group gathered around her throne.

"Where is the elixir of life?"

Maker's eyes grew wide under his bushy gray brows. He glanced at Donna, but she refused to meet his gaze. "I'll give it to you as soon as you let the prisoners go. They will wait for me at the door, and then we'll all leave together."

The Wood Queen hissed. "I have shown good faith—I gave you your human boy *and* the old magician. You have not yet proved to me you even have the elixir."

Donna swallowed. Okay, that was true. But Aliette had taken her friends in the first place—she'd replaced them with doubles and was willing to do anything in her quest to save her people. Still, there was something to be said for good faith.

Slowly, Donna reached into her pocket.

As soon as she moved, the hissing elves slid forward, closing the gap between them until she felt almost claustrophobic.

"Wait," she said. "I'm just showing it to you."

She felt cornered. They were so close to escaping, but they had one final—and potentially deadly—obstacle to overcome. Donna now knew that there was no way she could give the elves something so potent, no matter what doubts she had about the Order. None of that mattered; not if the elixir really *did* heal and create new life, or even bestow immortality on those who drank it. The whole situation seemed crazy, even with the upbringing she'd had—but then again, she'd seen a brass statue of a guy's head scream today. Her life had just reached a whole new level of crazy, and she wasn't going to take any chances.

She licked her dry lips and grasped the pouch inside her pocket. With her forefinger and thumb she squeezed once, quickly and with just enough pressure to achieve what she hoped... She only had one shot at this, and if she'd miscalculated even slightly, it was over for all of them. She held her breath as she carefully drew the vial out of the pouch, holding it up so that the moonlight glinted on the red liquid inside. It looked like it contained a tiny blood sample after a finger-stick test.

Maker lurched forward, horribly unsteady on his feet without his cane. "*No!* You can't give it to them, Donna."

Feeling hot guilt well up within her as Maker stumbled to his knees, Donna couldn't help thinking that the old alchemist's fear would help her case. Surely the Wood Queen couldn't doubt, now, that she really intended to hand over the elixir.

Her eyes pricked with tears of relief as she saw Aliette pass her dagger to a waiting wood elf so it could use the blade to free Navin's hands. Maker was pulled to his feet and dragged over to join Donna. He limped slowly toward her.

"Maker," she whispered as he reached her. She tentatively reached out to him and he gripped her velvet-clad hand in his own surprisingly strong fingers.

"It's good to see you, child. I just wish I knew what you have planned." His intelligent blue eyes seemed to look right inside her, and she had to resist the urge to throw her arms around him. "You do have a plan, don't you?" he continued under his breath.

"Trust me," was all she had time to say before turning to Navin, who was carefully picking his way across the undergrowth to reach her. The bruise on his face was starting to show more—purple and black against his brown skin—but his dark eyes were clear.

She ran to Navin and collapsed against his bony chest, tears running down her cheeks as he wrapped his arms around her. She buried her nose in his shoulder to better smell the familiar fake leather of his jacket. It was torn on one arm, but to see him standing there in one piece wearing it—to be holding him in her arms—made her so happy she could almost forget where they were and the danger they were still in.

"Donna," he said, his mouth resting against her hair. "Are you all right?"

She pulled away from him for a moment. "*Me*? I'm fine—what about *you*?"

"Dude, I am *so* much better now," he replied with feeling.

"Xan!" Donna called. "You have to get them back to the door—wait for me, but not for too long…" Her voice trailed off.

Xan's eyes flashed with barely suppressed anger. "I won't just 'wait' for you, Donna. If you don't arrive at the door within five minutes, I'm coming back for you."

Donna blew out a frustrated sigh. "You have to wait, Xan, that's the deal. You go on ahead—you'll need to help Maker—and I'll deal with the Wood Queen. Then I'll follow. It's simple." She lifted her chin as though daring anyone to argue with her.

Then Maker spoke, surprising them. "Donna, you don't *really* have the elixir, do you?" His tone was low, as though he was trying to speak only to her.

Donna met his concerned gaze. "Maker, you need to go with the others now."

"You do realize what would happen if they got hold of it," the alchemist continued, his voice rising with concern.

Actually, she thought, *I don't know. I don't know anything*. All she could do was trust her heart and hope that she'd made the right choice.

Her eyes and voice were steady as she looked at Navin. "Please help him along the Path," she said, indicating

Maker. "Xan will lead and open the door." She caught Xan's eye and nodded at him, hoping he would be able to get everyone to safety.

She didn't know what would happen after they'd gone, but she was determined that nobody else would be at risk because of her. Not again. This was her chance to make amends for everything that Navin had gone through.

Aliette's brittle voice cut through the air, making Donna jump. "You are to leave the Elflands and never return." She fixed Xan with her mossy glare. "I will take measures to ensure the door you have opened remains closed, *halfling*. Do not attempt to use the Old Paths again."

Donna saw Navin's curious glance at Xan and sighed, knowing that *if* they all got out of this, she would have a lot more explaining to do.

Xan reached for her hand and gave it a squeeze, trying to communicate something. Donna felt sadness weigh her down, but she couldn't let it stop her. She desperately wanted to say something to him—something significant about how she'd felt since their first meeting. But so much had happened and was *still* happening—it seemed like there just wasn't enough time. She wanted him to know how important he had become to her in just a matter of days, but her mouth didn't seem to be working properly. Their connection spoke of loss and pain, of being part of something greater than themselves, and of all the gifts they possessed, even though hidden under a mask of scars.

And then Nav hugged her and led Maker into the tunnel of darkly whispering leaves. Xan ran to catch up, looking back once and shooting her another of those fierce glances—she knew he was telling her *be careful, or else*.

So Donna Underwood stood alone, in the center of the Ironwood underneath the carnivorous sky, facing the Wood Queen and six of her twisted elves, as the moon peeked out from between the diminishing clouds.

Twenty

"G ive me the elixir," demanded the Wood Queen.
Donna began backing toward the edge of the clearing, trying to put as much distance between herself and the throne as possible.

"*Now!*"

Aliette's voice had that fingers-on-chalkboard quality that makes every hair on the back of your neck stand up. Donna cringed as her arms and hands filled with a terrible, stabbing pain; she clenched her fists and held her breath until the spasm passed. It seemed that the more energy the

Wood Queen expended, the more Donna's hands ached. She gritted her teeth and took another step back.

"It's right here, your majesty," she said, just barely able to get the words past her chattering teeth. She held out the vial with shaking fingers, terrified that at any moment the glass would crack. She continued shuffling backwards.

The queen's bottomless black eyes narrowed into cruel slits. "Where are you going?" she howled, the sound almost driving Donna to her knees. But she would not let herself be overpowered—she bit the inside of her mouth and tried to ignore the steady throb in her temples.

She waved the vial. "Here, take it."

At the Wood Queen's gesture, one of the elves scuttled forward, regarding Donna with its ancient eyes. It moved crablike, circling around her right-hand side, forcing her to turn with it in order to keep it safely within view. She extended her arm slowly, holding the vial in front of the creature, hoping that for *just one more second* nobody would notice the precious drops of liquid dribbling from the growing fracture in the casing.

As the elf suddenly moved closer, Donna took a deep breath and threw the vial across the clearing, as far and as hard as she could. Painfully aware that she had just tossed away generations of research and study, she watched as the glass spun in the moonlit sky and then fell into a scrubby patch of greenery. The wood elf scampered after it, and Donna turned and *ran* back down the tree-lined corridor, gasping as she tripped on a tree root and righted herself just in time. She was plunged into near darkness but still kept going, not caring when her hat flew off, not bothering to stop for it, just running and running along the ancient path, scattering dead leaves and twigs along the way. She ran faster than she'd ever thought possible—cold air sang in her throat and her chest felt stretched too tight. Whatever happened, she would have to start exercising regularly from now on. She tried not to think about what might be behind her, or whether or not she was being pursued.

Slowing her pace as she approached the end of the tunnel, she saw Xan waiting to ferry her through the door. He had already taken the others through.

"Are they coming?" he asked, gazing past her, his eyes wide and shining even in the dim light. His breath made little clouds in front of his face.

"I don't think so," she gasped, struggling to regulate her breathing.

Xan took a step back to make room for her, pulling her toward him to ensure that they stepped through the door together. He was clutching the familiar bundle of earth and twigs, dead leaves and moss, and she rested her midnight-blue glove on top of it, waiting for the dizzying sensation of moving-without-moving.

Then they were ducking out of the tiny clearing and crashing into the undergrowth, Donna still glancing behind them at the invisible door. Just because Xan had closed it and scattered the earth and leaves he'd been holding didn't mean the wood elves couldn't open it from their side.

But as they clambered through the brambles and Donna cursed the thorns scratching her cheeks, she began to think that maybe they had gotten away. Maybe they would be safe and could all just get into Xan's car and return to Ironbridge, going back to something close to a normal life (whatever that meant for any of them). She refused to think about what would happen when the Wood Queen found the broken vial.

She refused to allow herself to think about the consequences that she herself would face with the Order.

Xan grabbed her hand and pulled her onto the main path. They passed underneath a particularly heavy covering of ferns and branches where she couldn't see the moon at all. She stubbed her toe on a gnarled root and stopped for a moment, tugging on Xan's hand to make him wait.

"Are you okay?" he asked anxiously. "We need to keep moving—Navin and Maker will be waiting farther down. It's not far now."

Donna leaned down to re-tie her sneaker, glad for a moment to catch her breath. "How do they know the way?"

"Maker," Xan replied, simply.

Of course Maker would know the Ironwood, after all his years holding back the fey threat. Donna straightened up and pulled her coat more tightly around her. "I'm ready."

The words had only just left her mouth when she heard it again: the sound that haunted her nightmares and wouldn't leave her for as long as she lived: the otherworldly scream of the Skriker, ripping through her ears and vibrating in her body. The sound was much closer this time, but even if it wasn't, she felt attuned to it now, somehow—every shriek was bringing her closer to that awful memory.

No wonder the elves hadn't come after them, she thought. Why would they need to when the Wood Queen had loosed her pet on them?

Donna clutched Xan's arm, for a moment forgetting the strength in her hands, and gazed panic-stricken into his wide eyes. "Xan, we have to get out of here." Her voice trembled and she hated herself for her fear, but the ache in her arms reminded her why she was afraid. The terror was blinding-white in her mind, blocking out all other thoughts and any ability to move.

Xan was shaking her. "Come *on*, Donna, what are you standing there for?"

They ran, not caring about the sharp branches whipping at their faces, not caring which direction they ran in. Donna hoped they were staying on the main path, but she couldn't be sure. It was too dark and they were running too fast—the moon was hidden behind a sudden coating of thick cloud and she could only see the eerie silhouettes of tree trunks and clawed branches.

The nerve-shredding scream came at them from the left, and the next thing Donna knew she was knocked over, all the air driving out of her lungs as she smashed into Xan and landed on top of him. There was a confused moment when she wasn't sure whether he'd pushed her down to protect her, or if they had both just been blind-sided by the silent-running hellhound.

She pulled herself free, struggling to lever Xan's weight off her without hurting him with her strength. Her heart constricted when she saw thick blood oozing from a wide gash in his forehead. His face was gray, and the sticky blood was already congealing in his hair, glistening in a shaft of moonlight poking through the treetops.

The ground was littered with jagged rocks; he must have hit his head. She prayed that Xan was only uncon-scious. For a moment it was as though time had stopped—Donna didn't care about the Skriker, the wood elves, the elixir of life—all she could think about was Xan lying motionless on the ground. His arms had been around her, protecting her from the dark creature now breathing in deep grunts somewhere beyond the ring of trees, saving her from the worst of the fall. He had been unable to save himself while sheltering her.

Moaning in fear, Donna listened for signs of life, her ear close to Xan's pale lips. He lay so still and his cheek was cold—it reminded her of when she was a child, lean-ing over her father's body. Then she felt a warm whisper of breath touch her face. Flooded with relief, she was about to place her ear to Xan's chest, just to be certain, when the screeching started once more.

Donna put her hands over her ears as she tried to shut out the horrific noise. She crouched over Xan's body and found herself wondering whether the baying creature had changed much in all these years.

Strange, she thought, *the way the mind works when you're facing death.*

Dragging herself to her feet, Donna looked into the dimly lit forest. She had no idea where she was anymore—no clue where Navin or Maker were. Once again, she was alone with the Wood Monster. And this time her father wouldn't be coming to save her.

With a loud crack as it knocked down a fragile sapling, the Skriker leapt into view. Somehow, Donna thought it would seem smaller now that she was grown up, but the giant dog crouching before her was the size of a small horse. Donna slowly retreated, her eyes fixed on the black creature in front of her while she tried not to trip over Xan's prone form. Its yellow eyes glowed like sickly embers and smoke poured from its mouth and nostrils, stinking of bonfires. The trees lit up as it advanced on her, its crimson aura growing brighter by the second. The ground beneath its massive paws burned and shuddered.

The Skriker opened its jaws and screamed.

Blue flames burst from its mouth, licking the trunks of trees like a giant fiery tongue. Donna threw herself to the ground and rolled to the side, smashing her shoulder on the hard earth and her knee against a tree. Keeping her wary eyes on Xan, hoping the hellish dog either wouldn't notice him or would just think he was dead, she crawled onto her hands and knees and pulled herself up, using the tree for support. Her legs were shaking and her body ached but she pushed through the pain, remembering that terrified girl she'd once been. She allowed herself to think of her father, and glanced once more at Xan. *Not again*, she told herself. *Never again*.

She removed her gloves. The velvet material dropped to the ground as Donna stood, her back braced against the old tree. By the light of the moon she saw the Skriker's amber eyes rest on her as more smoke belched from its mouth.

Its shaggy black hide moved fluidly over its muscles as it lowered its head and charged toward her.

And suddenly, Donna was overwhelmed with a sense of complete calm—she was facing death, and yet there was a feeling of serenity flowing through her. Maybe it was just shock, but she would take strength where she could find it. She held her hands out in front of her and watched as the moon reflected off the silver lines flowing across and beneath her skin. The shimmering lattice that encapsulated her hands and arms was moving at a startling rate, winding around and around in a spiral motion that made her fingers numb.

Clenching her fists at the last moment, Donna turned her head away as the Skriker crashed into her and slammed her back against the tree. The burning creature's chest had driven into her hands, her silver fists plunging *through* its black fur and flesh and directly into its massive heart.

There was no blood, just blue flame—cold and unforgiving to human flesh, but powerless against Donna's magically enhanced arms. The cold iron lacing her skin and bones had sliced through the Skriker's fey hide like the sharpest knife. She collapsed under the weight of the dying creature. Its huge head flopped back on its neck as it tried to drag itself back onto its haunches, desperate to escape the agony she had inflicted on it.

Half-crushed and only semiconscious, Donna listened to the Skriker's dying breaths and felt a burst of pity for this thing that had maimed her as a child and killed her father. And instead of being angry with herself for thinking this way, she felt only acceptance. The creature was merely a tool of the Wood Queen, of that Donna was certain. It didn't know what it was doing; it was created simply to instill fear—and where fear didn't work, to kill. Compassion was a quality she knew Patrick Underwood valued highly, and she was glad to think that he might be proud of her.

Now, as she lay battered and bruised under the giant body of the Skriker, she knew what it was to destroy something yet also feel a sense of pity for it.

After several minutes, Donna managed to crawl out from beneath the creature's bulky frame, pushing hard with her shaking legs and rolling to the side as its giant head fell forward, tongue lolling out. She winced as she dragged herself through the still-burning embers scattered along the ground, the knees of her jeans not affording nearly enough protection. Just for a moment she wondered why there wasn't a minor forest fire, then remembered that the flames were of another world—of another time and place—and would not burn the same way Prometheus' gift did. This wasn't the fire of the alchemists.

Xan was just beginning to stir, moaning in pain as he turned his head. Donna scrambled to his side, wondering whether she could tear the lining out of her coat to make a bandage. Wasn't that what they did in movies? And then she realized she had the perfect bandage—the black velvet pouch that had held the elixir. She tore it open, ripping the seams with ease, and pressed the cloth gently to the wound on Xan's head, all the while urging him to lie still until help arrived. She was desperately banking on Navin and Maker finding them; otherwise, she would have to leave Xan here and try to find her way out of the Iron-wood in the dark. Even with the occasional glimpse of white moon, she doubted it would be easy. She was well and truly lost.

"Rest," she whispered to Xan, pulling his head onto her lap and stroking back his blood-matted hair. "You're bleeding."

"Donna." His voice was so faint she could hardly hear him.

"Shh," she repeated. "Don't try to talk."

Xan's eyes flickered open, the emerald light within them flashing briefly, then closed again. His head rolled to the side and he groaned.

"Please," Donna prayed. "Navin, please find us."

And just as she spoke these words aloud, she heard a distant voice. The voice was calling her name, and getting louder and louder.

"I'm here!" she called. She ran her fingers through Xan's hair again, reveling in the freedom of doing so without wearing her gloves, and wondering if she would get the chance to touch him like this when he was fully conscious. She leaned down and kissed his cheek. *I hope so*, she thought.

Navin burst through the undergrowth. "Donna, you're okay!" He looked at the half-conscious Xan lying in her lap. "What happened?"

She nodded in the direction of the Skriker's body, behind him, and couldn't help enjoying the expression of shock on her friend's face. "That, Navin, is a Skriker."

"*Was* a Skriker, don't you mean?" Awe radiated from his voice. "It sort of looks like a bear."

She shook her head and almost smiled. Navin could always make her smile and she loved him for that. "It's not a *bear*, Sharma. What kind of bears do they have on your planet?"

He ignored her and gazed at Xan for a long moment. "Did *he* kill it?"

"No," she said, lifting her chin and meeting his eyes. "It was me."

"Seriously?" Navin's expression was a complicated mixture of horror, disbelief, and...admiration.

"Yeah, seriously."

"Huh." He crouched down by the creature's body. "Pretty cool, Underwood."

Pride burst in her chest for the second time in the space of minutes.

"Pretty cool," Navin repeated. "And pretty *gross*."

Before she could throw a retort, Xan shifted against her and tried to lever himself into a sitting position.

"Hey, take it easy," Donna said, doing her best to keep him steady.

"I'm okay," Xan replied. And it actually seemed like he was, because the next moment, Alexander Grayson gently pushed away from her fussing hands and slowly began to stand. His hair was still matted with blood and he looked pretty dazed, but he was moving well enough, all things considered. Donna screwed up her face with confusion when she realized that the gash in his forehead looked almost closed.

She jumped to her feet—ignoring the wave of dizziness that almost planted her on her butt again—and touched Xan's face. It was still pretty dark … could she have been mistaken about his wound?

Navin was watching the two of them, which felt a little weird, but she couldn't worry about it right now. The gash had truly closed. Donna licked her thumb and rubbed crusted blood away from where the injury should have been, ignoring Xan's protests. How had he healed so quickly? Was it a faery thing?

She glared at him, unable to suppress a rising tide of suspicion. He himself had told her there was still a lot she didn't know about him, and now here she was, getting pissed off about that very fact. *What was wrong with her?* She should just be happy he was okay. Donna took a steadying breath and tried not to sound accusing.

"You were bleeding like crazy a minute ago, Xan. Now there's no cut here."

He frowned, looking genuinely puzzled about why she was angry. "Maybe it wasn't as bad as you thought it was?"

She narrowed her eyes. "It was bad. Trust me on that. It was pretty bad."

He ran his fingers over where the wound should have been. "I don't know what happened, I swear." He glanced over at Navin. "Is she always this damn suspicious?"

Navin smirked, and the moment of connection between the two guys would have been a relief to Donna if it weren't for the fact they were bonding over dissing *her*.

And then a thought struck her. Not just any thought, either. This was a big one—potentially huge and apparently life-saving. She gazed at the piece of blood-drenched material in her hand, material that had originally held the vial of elixir.

The vial that she had crushed while it was *still inside* the pouch.

Could there have been a drop of elixir on the material? If even the tiniest trickle of liquid had escaped the damaged vial before she'd removed it from the pouch, it would have soaked into the lining. Which meant that maybe Xan was telling the truth after all—maybe he really *didn't* have magical fey healing abilities. Maybe Donna had accidentally healed him with a legendary alchemical compound that she wasn't even sure she believed in.

Until now.

Navin touched her shoulder. "Donna, what is it?"

She licked her lips and shook her head, trying to smile. "Nothing. Don't worry, it's nothing."

Yeah, like either of them would buy that.

But Donna didn't know what to think of any of this right now, and they needed to get out of here. Xan was okay, which was what mattered.

Then Xan abruptly frowned at Navin. "Hey, where's the old guy?"

Navin indicated over his shoulder. "Not far. He's waiting on a tree stump by the path."

Donna breathed a sigh of relief. "The path's nearby?"

Navin nodded. "Sure. You almost made it."

You almost made it. His innocent words echoed in her mind and Donna couldn't bring herself to reply. They *had* made it; everybody was safe. She'd achieved her goal: she'd saved her best friend's life and retrieved Maker. She'd even destroyed the creature that had decimated her family, ten years before.

But at what cost?

The first light of morning was just beginning to peek through the clouds, bathing the treetops in an ethereal silver glow. They had met the Wood Queen's deadline. Donna tried to push aside her fears and concentrate on the fact that they had won. But somehow the victory felt hollow, no matter how relieved she was to see Navin smiling at her as he turned toward the path.

Glancing surreptitiously at Xan, impossibly invigorated considering all that they'd been through, she bit her lip and wondered how the hell she was going to explain all this to her aunt.

Navin still hasn't told me about his time with the wood elves. I know he understands more about my life now, about the nightmares I've had for so many years, but I wish his understanding hadn't come at such a horrible price. I hope he will talk to me about it, one day—I can't help worrying, and he's been so quiet.

Simon Gaunt took great pleasure in returning my charm bracelet. He'd found it inside his oratorium, right next to the smashed incubator.

Way to get caught red-handed.

Aunt Paige was furious that I'd put myself in such danger, and she was the most emotional I've ever seen her. She actually cried when we got back to the Frost Estate. But I have a bad feeling that her tears weren't all about my safety.

I was proven right when Quentin Frost set a date for the hearing.

Yeah, me…Donna Underwood…who never asked to be born into this crazy magical life, is being hauled in front of a panel of alchemists to answer for my actions. They aren't using the word "crimes," but they might as well. Nobody listens to me when I tell them I had to save Navin. Why would they care? He's just a commoner, after all. But they're not even listening to Maker. At least he isn't treating me like a criminal.

So, I'm grounded until the hearing. I spend all my time reading and re-reading emails from Xan, since they've confiscated my cell phone. He keeps me going, and he signs every letter with a kiss.

Acknowledgments

First of all, there would be no published book if it wasn't for my incredible agent, Miriam Kriss. You're the glue that holds my career (and sanity!) together—thank you for everything. My thanks also go to Heather Baror Shapiro for being *The Iron Witch*'s champion overseas.

Thank you to all of my wonderful publishers and editors. In the U.S.: Brian Farrey for giving new writers a chance and for helping to make this book so much better; Lisa Novak for the amazing cover, which I loved from the very first moment; Sandy Sullivan for her keen eye and sound judgment; Marissa Pederson and all the hardworking booklovers at Flux. Thanks so much to everyone at Random House Children's Books in the U.K. for giving me such a tremendous opportunity. In particular, I am grateful to Annie Eaton, Clare Argar, Lauren Bennett, Jessica Clarke, Emily van Hest, and Trish De Souza. Thanks also to the super-cool Adiba Oemar at Random House Children's Books in Australia, as well as the whole team at RHCB "Down Under."

To the Deadline Dames, I still find it hard to believe I'm part of such an amazing group of authors. Thanks to each of you: Devon, Jackie, Jenna, Keri, Lili, Rachel, Rinda, and Toni. Dames rock!

Thank you to my writing BFFs who have been there since Day One: Brian Kell, Chandra Rooney, Tricia Sullivan, and Reneé Sweet. Not only do you keep me going through the tough times and celebrate the good stuff with me, you have each helped me to become a better writer.

Thanks to ALL of my LiveJournal friends, as well as to the wider online world I'm proud to be a part of. In particular I must thank Ana Grilo, Liz and Mark de Jager, Stacia Kane, Caitlin Kittredge, Tessa Gratton, Richelle Mead, Tiffany Trent, and Ariana Valderrama. Thank you to Trisha Telep for believing in my work early on and encouraging my addiction to coffee. I am especially grateful to Rhona Westbrook and Maria Signorelli, whose early critiques undoubtedly improved *The Iron Witch*.

My thanks to Midori Snyder for writing the essay about the "Armless Maiden" tales that provided the initial spark for Donna's story. To Jonathan Carroll: your words inspired me way back when I was "sweet sixteen" just as they do today, so many years later.

Last, but by no means least, thank you to my family and all of my Real Life friends, who have helped shape the person I've become. And especially to Maralyn Mahoney (my lovely mum) and Vijay Rana (my very own Navin): you have supported my dreams and pushed me to tell my stories. I can't thank you enough.

The Girl with Silver Hands:
The Making of *The Iron Witch*
by Karen Mahoney

The Iron Witch is the result of almost four years' dreaming, researching, and writing. If there were a recipe – or indeed a spell – that I could offer you that would reproduce the final work, it would involve a huge list of ingredients, along with a complex method and an invocation. Even before the long path to publication, there was always a central idea: a girl with silver hands, the friend she loves and is forced to save (loosely based on my own Real Life best friend), and a life of dark secrets that she wants to escape from.

Okay, so that's three ideas . . .

In 2007, I read a beautiful essay by fantasy author and folklore expert Midori Snyder, called "The Armless Maiden and the Hero's Journey" (reprinted in the online *Journal of Mythic Arts*, Winter 2006). This piece inspired me like nothing else had in years, and I immediately started trying to re-imagine how a YA urban fantasy novel might incorporate the powerful themes of the Armless Maiden narratives from around the world. There are many versions of the tale, and I am by no means an authority – but I did spend a lot of time tracking down obscure references and reading translations of the different stories, and I hope to touch on some of that in this essay.

Even though they all tell a similar story, there are a wide range of titles given to the tales: "The Armless Maiden," "The Handless Maiden," "The Girl/Woman/Maiden Without Hands," "Doña Bernarda," "Rising Water, Talking Bird and Weeping Tree," "Olive,"

"The Girl with Silver Hands," and many more. The stories share many common elements, including the loss of hands or arms for the girl or woman – in violent circumstances – and the eventual "regrowth" of the limbs as she slowly regains her power and independence. In most versions, there is a halfway point in the story where the maiden meets a prince or a king who falls in love with her despite her disability, ordering a member of his royal court – sometimes a magician – to build a replacement pair of hands for his new bride. These magical hands and arms are usually made of silver.

Although there is much to discuss about the depth and hidden layers of meaning within the Handless Maiden stories, it was this striking visual element that fired my imagination when I first read about it. I wondered how I could create a modern-day heroine with 'silver hands' and the power to transform her own life. How could I make that fit in with a contemporary or urban setting? When I hit upon the notion of having my protagonist's hands and arms coated with silver tattoos that, when looked at quickly, might make it look as though her hands were made of solid metal, I knew I was onto something. And when I made the leap to realizing that Donna's tattoos should be made of iron rather than silver, I found the crucial link between the alchemists and the faeries.

Speaking of the fey . . . they first made an appearance in one of the crazy dreams I had during an intense two week period when ideas just wouldn't stop coming. One of those dreams showed me a young girl – still just a child – running barefoot through a wintering forest, pursued by a pack of screaming monsters. Those monsters became the wood elves of *The Iron Witch*, and the creature that almost mortally wounded Donna became the Skriker (the "Wood Monster" in her imagination), one of the legendary Black Dogs of English folklore.

Yes, I admit, I'm guilty of mixing my lore – but I believe if you dare to do so *consciously*, and you come up with some reasonable justifications for the liberties you take, then you're kind of okay. Mostly. You also might have noticed that part of *The Iron Witch* was born out of a DREAM. We will not mention anything more about that, suffice it to say that I can only hope *my* "dream book" is even a thousandth as successful as a Certain Other Paranormal Book Inspired by a Dream.

In many versions of the traditional Armless Maiden stories, the girl is a victim of her own family. Sometimes this is due to an outright betrayal, but it can also be caused by a tragic mistake in which the father or brother is tricked by an evil force (often the Devil) into sacrificing the maiden's hands. In the interpretation I chose to use, we see that Donna's loss comes as an indirect result of her family's lifelong affiliation with the alchemists. If she were not a daughter of the Order, it seems unlikely that she would ever have been attacked by the fey in the first place. Of course, we don't yet know why that happened . . . though I promise you'll find out in the next book. (Not that I'm plugging the sequel. *cough*)

I think that Donna Underwood's story (and it's no coincidence that I named her "Underwood," by the way, with its obvious woodland connotations and subtle play on the word "Underworld") is the story of a seventeen year-old girl who must grow from childhood to adulthood far too quickly. Yes, she has experienced tragedy, but she doesn't wallow in it. She is proactive and wants to change her life: *transformation*, as she tells Navin, is important to the alchemists.

That theme of transformation is as important to my own "Girl with Silver Hands" story as it is in the folklore I researched. The Handless Maiden is often seen as an outsider – something that

Donna truly understands at the start of the book. She has felt like a "freak" for the last ten years of her life, and must learn to look upon her iron tattoos as a gift if she is ever truly to gain the freedom she so desperately desires.

This theme is taken up in what is perhaps my favorite retelling of the tale, the one recounted by Dr. Clarissa Pinkola Estés in her seminal work, *Women Who Run With the Wolves*. Dr. Estés explains that "The Handless Maiden" tale is truly that of the heroine's "Test of Endurance." There's a line in her wonderfully Jungian interpretation that resonates with me and feels very true for *The Iron Witch*:

> *"The story pulls us into a world that lies far below the roots of trees."*

I didn't read Dr. Estés' book until long *after* I'd written the first draft of my novel, but now that I can carefully examine her version of "The Handless Maiden"—and the many-layered interpretation of the tale that she offers – I see so many parallels. I don't mean in terms of the events, because those are very different. But Estés equates the tale with a sort of shamanic journey, including the requisite descent into the underworld and the physical transformation of the heroine. *Sacrifice* is a central theme – and it's a big theme I plucked out of that mystical melting pot of universal archetypes we writers tune in to from time to time.

Okay, that's enough New Age or "woo woo" references for now. The next ingredient that went into my cauldron when I was first stirring up the idea for *The Iron Witch* was alchemy. I've been fascinated by the idea of alchemists for many years, and started seriously researching it about six years ago. I used to work in an occult bookstore and had easy access to some wonderful resources, including antiquarian texts not readily available elsewhere. I've always loved that the historical alchemists seem to have taken themselves so seriously. And it's interesting that many of them operated in secret, afraid of the ridicule that would befall them if it was known how they liked to dabble in one of the more mystical branches of esoteric study.

Alchemy is an ancient art – centuries old – and there have been branches of it all over the world. There are some pretty far-out theories as to how the alchemists came upon their information, encompassing everything from demons to Egyptian gods to channelled angels and even alien technology. It's hard to believe that alchemy was actually a precursor to today's study of chemistry, but there was a lot of method, ritual, and painstaking note-taking involved in their pseudo-scientific experiments, even back in the sixteenth century. I tried to get a flavor of that into *The Iron Witch*, but it would've been easy to overdo it and I had to be careful (there's just way too much fascinating source material). Also, I really wanted to make the subject my own, for my book, so I created my four alchemical Orders from scratch. I had a great deal of fun doing that.

All right, then. So far we have the Handless Maiden, wood elves, and the alchemists. The final major ingredient of my story came from a sudden flash of inspiration, the kind that usually hits writers at the worst possible time and has us scrambling for a notebook – or a handy receipt – *anything* just so long as we get it written down before we forget it! This insight came to me as an image, basically, and whenever happens I make sure to take it seriously, since I'm not usually that artistic in the visual sense.

I pictured a teenage boy – or perhaps a young man – with dark blond hair covering his face, sitting bent over and quietly weeping. He was strong and determined, I knew that much, and yet he still couldn't stop the tears from falling (though perhaps that was part of his strength). He had been physically mutilated, and as a result he'd lost something he felt he couldn't live without.

Cheery, huh? My brain is a very strange place to hang out – I don't recommend it.

Obviously, this lonely guy with secrets of his own became Xan, and from very early on, I knew almost as much about him as I did about Donna. Alexander Grayson had a lot to tell me, so I made sure to listen and take notes.

Once I had these major building blocks in place – the folklore, the magic, and the love interest – I merely had to add them to Donna and Navin's friendship, and to the constant battle Donna fights to fit into Nav's "normal" world, and I was all set to cause some chaos in my characters' lives (picture me rubbing my hands together in Authorly Anticipation.)

I hope you've enjoyed visiting the world of Ironbridge in my story, and that you'll come back again soon. There are a lot more secrets to uncover – and it wouldn't be any fun if I couldn't share it with you. Thanks for reading!

Karen Mahoney
LONDON, 2011